Big Rucking Disaster

RUCKED BY YOU

GABBI GREY

Big Rucking Disaster

Johnnie

I'm the hooker (no, not that kind) for the Vancouver Orcas rugby squad, and my teammates are like family. They're nosy like family too, worrying about me, even though I pretend I'm doing fine. But off the pitch, I'm stuck in a bad relationship, struggling to get along with Carly. I hope that volunteering for a local high school might make me feel I'm doing some good in the world. And the kids are great, but it's Coach Yardley Morrison who feels like someone who might change my life. One look into his dark-brown eyes, and suddenly I'm wondering if I can make different, better choices.

Yardley

I'm convinced Johnnie Leclerc will just swoop in, sign autographs, get the kids excited, and then abandon them. Like my bastard ex-husband. So I play it smart and keep my distance from the sexy, but straight—remember he's straight, Yardley—rugby star. But as weeks go by, the more he keeps his promises to the kids, staying patient and kind with them, the more attractive I find him. I know better than to hit on a guy like that, of course. Except every now and then, our gazes meet, and I don't think I'm imagining the heat I see.

Big Rucking Disaster is a 29k word opposites attract, age-gap, bi-awakening, interracial gay sports novella with a by-the-book coach and the hell-raising hooker who wants to change his ways.

multimedia, audio, or other medium. We support the right of humans to control their artistic works.

No generative AI was used in the creation of this book.

Edits by ELF

Cover by The Cover Fling

Dedication

To my other dad—having you in my life is a beautiful thing.

Contents

Prologue

Johnnie

"**Y**ou were amazing, baby." Carly feathered her hand through my hair.

I hated when she did that.

Both called me *baby* and ran her hand through my hair. Her fingernails always snagged on it, pulling at the roots.

I glanced around to see if any of my teammates were paying attention.

Nope.

Isaiah was making googly eyes at his man, Travis.

Roger had his arm around his twelve-year-old daughter Cassandra's shoulders. Travis had brought the young woman to the match since her mom, Becca, was home with baby Kristine Angelique. Before long, Becca would be back in the stands. Having kids never held her back.

Jason's fiancée, Sonya, grinned as she kept Walter, Jason's parrot, on her shoulder. She'd snuck the salty-mouthed bird into the stadium, supposedly behind security's backs.

They didn't care. Just like they'd let Carly in when she wasn't really supposed to be here.

"Are we going out with the team?" Carly's green eyes shone. She loved spending time with the team. She loved being one of the wives and girlfriends. What she didn't understand—but what had become incredibly apparent to me recently—was just how much everyone else despised her.

Oh, they'd never say so. My teammates and their families would never do anything so cruel. But Isaiah's Travis had asked an innocent question about why she hadn't been invited to their housewarming since everyone was supposed to be there.

The worst part was, I hadn't even considered inviting her.

When she found out, she was furious.

I thought that might be the end of us.

In fact, I sort of hoped it might be.

Nope.

She'd redoubled her efforts to get invited everywhere and to be in the middle of everything.

Is she doing this because she cares about you, or because she wants to be on the in *with the team?*

I didn't have an answer for that.

"Carly?"

"Hmm?" Finally, she pulled her gaze away from the other players and their partners.

"I have a headache. I think I just want to go home."

"Oh sure, baby." Again with the feathering. "You took a hard hit. Francine didn't do a concussion protocol on you. I think she should have."

Irritation rose in me. Carly was forever questioning Francine's treatments. Our trainer was the best in the league, and we were damn lucky to have her. I kept waiting for a pro hockey, soccer, or football team to poach her. She loved rugby, though, and didn't mind the Vancouver rain.

"I didn't hit my head, so she didn't need to do anything. It's just a little buzz, but it'll get worse if I don't lie down."

"Sure. I'll take care of you—"

"No, that's not necessary. Really."

"Baby, of course it—"

"Jesus Christ, Carly." I pulled away. "Give it a rest. Give it a god-damn rest."

"Hey, everything okay?" Roger gently eased Cassandra into Travis's arms and approached Carly and me. "There are little ears."

Speaking of ears...mine burned. "I'm sorry." I faced Roger. "My bad." I pivoted to my girlfriend. "I've had a rough day, and I need to be alone. I'll, uh, call you."

Before anyone could respond, I beat a path to the exit.

Chapter One

Yardley

"Aw, fuck." I eyed my phone. "Today? It has to be today?"

Hugo gazed up from his coffee. "Today is always today, my friend. That's the way the world works. Oh, did I show you Midnight's latest trick?" He queued up his phone and hit play.

I watched while Midnight the Samoyed twirled on her back paws. Kind of adorable. "How did a white dog get the name Midnight? And it looks like she's shedding." I spotted some of her notoriously thick fur flying.

"The family we rescued her from named her. I think the kids had a hand in that. And yeah, she's molting. It's March, spring is on the way, and she's...shedding like crazy."

"Your friends are watching her next week, right?"

Hugo grinned. "Renee and Cope, yeah. She'll get to play with the twins, Matthew and Scarlett, who are getting mighty big." He swiped to another picture of the toddlers. His best friend and her husband had become parents after years of trying, and their joy at the antics of their twins was visible in all the photos Hugo shared. "I can't wait to see Grindstone perform. Axel's been away for three weeks now." He pouted.

"And yet you've survived." Hugo's rockstar fiancé was on tour right now with his band. The journey was ending with a big performance at Massey Hall in Toronto next week.

"I miss him."

"You're marrying him in less than a month."

"Well, there is that." He grinned. "And you're still standing up for me, right?"

I'd been surprised at the invitation. Since my divorce, though, I'd grown closer to Hugo. My ex...well, the less said, the better. Still, I'd have thought Hugo would pick Renee. With the twins, though, she didn't want to commit. "For sure."

Axel's bandmate and best friend Ed, was standing up for him.

They were opting for a small ceremony with just close friends. Hugo's parents were *not* invited, and Axel didn't have any blood family around. What the men had were Hugo's sister and her kids, as well as Axel's bandmates and a select few of Hugo's teaching friends. Found family. In some cases, far more important than blood.

The bell rang.

Hugo pocketed his phone. "Oh, hey. What was the *fucking today* about?" He slung his messenger bag over his shoulder as we prepared to leave the staff room—him for his music room and me for the gym.

"I've got a rugby player coming to speak to the students."

"What's wrong with that? I love when guests come and speak to the kids. Reinforces what I'm telling them but that they ignore because it's coming from me. And gives me a break from teaching." He grinned yet again.

Damn guy was happy all the fucking time.

Not that he was yucking my yum, but I wasn't as gloriously happy. I wasn't in love. I was newly divorced and just a little bitter. "This guy? Captain of Vancouver's Orcas. Big showoff. Huge social media presence." Damn attractive, gorgeous girlfriend, and probably stand-offish. Probably thought he was better than us just working as physical education teachers.

"Johnnie..." Hugo snapped his fingers.

"Johnnie Leclerc." I squinted. "How do you know him?"

"The local news did a segment about them. The team, I mean. How they're on this winning streak, but Montréal keeps breaking it. They're headed to national finals, if they beat Calgary and Winnipeg—which should be easy. If Montréal beats Toronto and Halifax, then the Orcas are against their archrivals again."

I scratched my stubbled chin. "I didn't know any of that. I've been focused on the Canucks this month." Vancouver's professional hockey team was actually doing really well, and it looked like they might make the playoffs. Undoubtedly, they'd lose at some point. It'd been over thirty years since a Canadian team had hoisted Lord Stanley's Cup. That drought was almost as old as I was. I'd been all of seven when the Canadiens won in '93. I wasn't overly optimistic about Canada's chances. I was a diehard Canuck fan until they lost for the season—then I'd cheer any and all Canadian teams who advanced.

"You know the Canucks aren't going to win."

"Of course I do."

"Fair. Later." He scurried out of the room while I was a fraction slower.

Louella had the basketball squad this morning and then ninth-grade girls. I got ninth-grade boys. Yay, fun. Marginally better than eighth grade—but not by much.

I wandered into the gym as Louella gave the girls a pep talk. The teacher was petite, with spikey red hair, deep-brown eyes, plenty of curves, and a wicked sense of humor. At the end of the chat, the girls sprinted for the showers while my co-teacher headed my way. She grinned. "Johnnie Leclerc, eh?"

"Last period. Grade Twelve." We taught that grade as mixed, so Johnnie would be sharing his wisdom with twenty-two wisecracking kids who wanted out of high school so badly they could taste it. A couple of girls and three of the boys loved rugby. We didn't have a squad at our school, but Greta played on a local team, and Kenji was hoping to get scooped up next year by a semi-pro team. I was trying to encourage him, all the while knowing sports were brutal.

"I wish I could be there. I'm at Central with the badminton team."

"It's great to get them out of the school for once."

"Small squad with great potential. Underrepresented sport in our school."

The bell rang again, and a gaggle of girls sprinted from the changing room to their homerooms.

I sighed as I unpacked my messenger bag. Midterm report cards were due soon, and I had a couple of students who thought my class was optional. They were going to find out quickly how I felt about that.

As with most Mondays, the day passed in a blur of kids, sports, drama, and comedy.

Hugo and I ate lunch together as he spoke about a violin player in his class who was showing huge potential. His enthusiasm couldn't be understated as he carried on about the young woman and how the money that flowed into the school after the scandal was helping tremendously.

The scandal.

In a moment of pique, Hugo's ex-husband, upon seeing Hugo with Axel Townsend, his former student, claimed Hugo and Axel had been involved in an affair when Axel was a teenager.

Total bullshit. I'd known Hugo back then, and he'd never looked at his student that way. He'd recognized talent and had nurtured it, but he sure as shit never looked at Axel as a potential sex partner.

Gross.

But douchebag ex-husband's allegations had to be investigated, and Axel and Hugo found themselves under a lot of scrutiny.

Hugo hired a damn good lawyer who uncovered asshole ex was actually up to his neck in fraud. He'd been arrested, Hugo had come off suspension, money had flowed in from people outraged at the school's arbitrary treatment of him, and now, he and Axel were getting married.

Through it all, my friend never wavered in his dedication to his students. For both of us, teaching was a vocation. A calling. We'd both chosen to work in one of the poorest neighborhoods in Vancouver because we believed in what we were doing.

As we rose from lunch, he gave me another long look. "Johnnie isn't your ex."

I snorted. "I should hope not. My ex was very gay."

"Johnnie's got a girlfriend."

"I am aware."

"Maybe don't judge him before you meet him?"

"He's going to come here, show off, sign a few autographs for adoring students, and then take off. Guys like that aren't in it for the hard work—they're in it for the glory."

"And what did I just say about not judging him? Especially for his looks."

"Ah." Because Johnnie looked a lot like my ex—golden blond, blue eyes, and a killer jawline. "I got taken in by looks. That won't happen again."

Hugo snickered. "Right. Just like I tried to tell myself that grown-up Axel wasn't my type."

"You were never interested in me." I puffed out my chest.

The truth was, we'd been fast friends, but that was it. Although I was Black, like Axel, Hugo had never seen me as a potential mate. Plus, we'd both been married when we'd met.

Ironically, both to assholes.

He'd ditched the ex long before I had. To my shame and regret.

"Later." Hugo waved and strode off.

I straggled back to the gym. I was accustomed to the funky smell. Like some kind of home.

Nicholas'd always insisted I shower before coming home because of what he referred to as *the stench of pubescent children*.

That should've been a hint he didn't want kids.

I figured that out way too late. Now, at thirty-nine, I didn't figure I'd ever have any of my own. So I'd make the best of what I had.

The grade-eleven boys after lunch were quite a crew. They wanted to play basketball all the time. I tried to explain we were here for all kinds of physical activity, but that often fell on deaf ears.

Today, with my mind on Johnnie Leclerc, I let most of them work on free throws.

I snagged three uninterested kids, and we went to the other end of the gym and practiced passing volleyballs. Tatum showed potential as a volleyball player, and I had hopes he'd make captain of the squad next fall in his senior year.

"Hey!" A cry came from the other end of the gym.

A volleyball smacked me on the head because, of course, I'd turned my head.

"Oh shit, Coach, I'm sorry." Tatum ran after the volleyball.

I pressed a hand to my temple. Yeah, that hurt. Still, I had work to do. "What's going on?" I stalked across the court to find two students glaring at each other.

"He tried to knock me over." Jared pointed.

Rudy shrugged.

I arched an eyebrow. All the while, my temple throbbed and my brain was starting to hurt.

"Look—"

"Quitting time!" Louella stepped out of the office. "You've got a guest arriving soon."

All the pipsqueaks ran for the changing room—Rudy and Jared leading the way. *Hopefully, they'll behave in the showers.*

Tatum hung back with the volleyball in his hands. "I'm so sorry—"

I waved him off. "Absolutely not your fault. I lost focus." I eyed the changing room. "Just one of those things, okay?"

He bounced the ball. "Who's the guest?"

"Johnnie Leclerc. He's a rugby player."

Tatum rolled his eyes. "The *up-and-coming sport*."

Rugby had been around about twenty-five years longer than volleyball, but I got Tatum's meaning. Two very different skill sets. Not his speed—at all. He loved the elegance of the white ball sailing through the air. He loved the lack of physical contact with the opposite team.

"Johnnie's at the front reception. I'll go grab him!" And just like that, Louella was gone.

Tatum regarded me for just one moment. "Is he good-looking?"

"Yes."

"Is he a good guy?"

"I hope so."

"Okay. See you tomorrow." With that, he sauntered to the changing room.

I went in search of an ice pack.

Chapter Two

Johnnie

L ouella, the phys-ed teacher, was an absolutely affable woman. Her wedding ring put me at ease in a way few things did these days. I wasn't as interested in playing the field as I had been not so long ago. After all, I had a gorgeous girlfriend, adoring fans, and plenty of adulation.

"We're so appreciative that you're willing to speak to our grade-twelve students." The petite woman hustled me down the hall, through the crowds of students.

I was taller than most of them—which wasn't a surprise. I was a bit leaner than most hookers in the league, but my strength was legendary. If one wanted to win a scrum, they needed me on their team. "It's my pleasure. Isaiah, my teammate, teaches high school. He's been telling me I need to get out into the community more." His exact words had been something like *you need to give back, and sitting around all day on your ass isn't doing that*. Or something to that effect.

"The kids are so excited. Coach Morrison says two have real potential."

"Coach Morrison?"

"Our other physical-education teacher. He's got the mixed grade-twelve class this afternoon. They're a rowdy bunch, but with good hearts."

Some kids who took physical education all the way through school did so because they wanted an adjacent career. Others took it because, generally, the class was easier than some academics. *Yeah, that was me.* I'd excelled at most sports and had loved my gym class. Now, I regretted not having tried harder in my academic classes. Thirty-one, and I worked a courier gig when I wasn't playing. Compared to Isaiah's teaching, I lacked...gravitas.

"In here." Louella led me into the school's gymnasium.

Ah, high school. Nothing quite smelled like it. I'd graced locker rooms for almost twenty years, and secondary schools just had a distinct odor.

A circle of chairs around center court caught my attention as I followed Louella to the group.

"Mr. Leclerc, this is our grade-twelve class. And this is the teacher, Mr. Morrison."

Mr. Morrison stood. *Okay, perhaps not what I was expecting. Except, who was I expecting?* My gym teacher had topped six-four and carried a significant amount of weight around his midsection. Former defensive liner for the BC Lions—Vancouver's football team.

In contrast, Mr. Morrison was...short. Barely over five-seven, if I had to guess. Whippet-lean. Yet clearly some muscles under his T-shirt. His dark-brown eyes assessed me.

I tried not to squirm under the scrutiny. The man was...hot. All dark skin, shaved head, and something indefinable. I wasn't into guys.

but I suspected Isaiah would find him attractive. This teacher had a similar build to my teammate's fiancé, Travis. I extended my hand. "Johnnie Leclerc."

Something flickered in his eyes as he extended his hand. "Coach Morrison. These are my students. Why don't you have a seat, and we can get started?" He pointed to a seat across the circle from him.

So he can keep an eye on me? I offered a wide grin. "Sounds great." I dropped my bag to the ground and sat. I wore my team jersey with a pair of khakis in deference to the Vancouver rainy, cold, miserable day. On the field, I wouldn't have hesitated to wear my shorts. Nothing deterred me from playing hard and fast. "So, before we start, maybe we can go around the circle, and each student can tell me something about themself." I had a great memory and would be able to remember all the names and whatever each student said.

"Oh." Coach Morrison frowned. "That's not really why..." He trailed off. "Sure, okay." He glanced at the kids. "Maybe something that's not too personal."

I'd never considered the students might reveal some deep, dark secret. I just wanted to get a sense of the kids and their aspirations.

Madison went first. She spoke about wanting to be a trainer for a pro team and how cool it was that Francine was the trainer for the Orcas.

I was damn impressed.

The kids who followed showed varying levels of interest in rugby. Some not at all—George spoke of hockey with reverence. Some with a great deal—Kenji enthused about wanting to make the Orcas team when he graduated high school. Greta was already playing for a local women's team, and she certainly had the build and attitude to be a great 15s player.

I loved my 15s.

Once we'd gone around the circle, Coach Morrison met my gaze. "Perhaps you can share the good and the bad of being a professional athlete?"

"Sure. The good? I love rugby more than life itself, and I get to play and get paid. The bad? Professional athletes don't get paid nearly as much money as you might think. Sure, pro baseball, hockey, and football players do well—on teams that are associated with the NHL, Major League Baseball, and the NFL. Some soccer teams as well. Most of the rest of us? Well, I've got a part-time job so I can pay the rent."

"What do you do?" Greta leaned in.

"Courier. Several days a week, I courier documents on a bicycle for law firms around the downtown core. The job isn't as lucrative as it once was because people can sign many documents over the internet, but there are still some things that have to be done the old-fashioned way. Sometimes I also pick up other business stuff. But let me tell you, cycling around downtown is dangerous, and I don't recommend it."

"But it's a good workout." Kenji slapped his thighs. "Quadriceps."

"And glutes." I attempted to jiggle my butt.

Coach's eyebrow arched.

I didn't pout.

Well, much.

"How often do you work out?" Juniper hadn't seemed all that keen when introducing themselves, but they brightened now.

So I went on to explain about my training schedule—how often I worked out with the team or by myself. I also veered into nutrition. Admitting I didn't always eat healthy, but that certain nutrients were important, and I was careful with supplements.

"How about concussions?" Greta gestured to her head. "I got knocked around once. I passed protocol, but my mom got super worried."

"She's right to worry. Rugby's a dangerous sport. All that body contact and no protective gear."

"Unlike hockey." George grinned.

"And football." Kenji rolled his eyes. "Wimps."

"Hey!" His schoolmate apparently didn't take kindly to that.

"I meant football players—"

"Hey!" This time, a rather large teenager, Moose, crossed his arms. Defensive tackle. Built like a brick shithouse, as my mate Jason would say.

"I think we can bring it down a notch." Coach caught the gaze of each of the kids. "Rugby's a very dangerous sport. As are many others. Perhaps you can take us through concussion protocol?" He stared at me with intense and laser-focused eyes.

"Sure. Something I'm way too familiar with." I took them through the entire protocol, including all the steps the doctors would take before deciding if I was concussed or not. "Three times. I don't recommend it."

"What about chronic traumatic encephalopathy?" Madison asked that question. Although athletic, she'd made it clear she wanted to be a trainer and not an athlete.

"CTE's a danger anytime you get knocked around. Obviously, the more concussions you have, the more likely you are to get it. It can only be diagnosed after death."

"That's why some athletes are arranging to donate their bodies when they die." George puffed out his chest.

Watch him. Kid's...a bit morbid.

"That's true. I've arranged for that as well. It's good to have a will and a medical directive when you play pro sports. I mean, those things are good to have anyway. I sure didn't think about it growing up, but now when I risk myself every week? I want to make sure people know what I want." *God, now I sound morbid.*

"Have you ever had a red card?" George again.

"Once. I have to say that wasn't my proudest moment. I accidentally hit a guy in the throat with my arm. Honest mistake—I thought he was turning one way, and he turned another. But I could've caused serious damage. There's no excuse for that, and I got turfed. I try really hard not to get them, though. I don't even like spending time in the sin bin." I rolled my eyes.

Everyone laughed.

Except Coach.

I don't know how to reach him. To assure him I'm one of the good ones. He appeared ready to boot me at any moment. Where was his antipathy coming from?

"Do we have enough time to try a couple of throws?"

"Yes!" Kenji leapt up. "I want to show you my moves."

George rolled his eyes. "Try doing it backwards in skates."

Coach rose. "We have a couple of minutes before the final bell."

We all folded our chairs and put them in a pile against the wall.

I pointed to George and Kenji. "I'm going to teach you how to throw behind your back while moving down the field."

"Dumbest game ever."

"George." The warning came from Coach.

"What? You can't move forward, you have to move sideways. It takes for-freaking-ever to get anywhere." He put his hands on his hips.

"I know, isn't it great?" I grinned.

Kenji high-fived me.

We were off.

Chapter Three

Yardley

"Are you all right?" Johnnie stared into my eyes. He leaned in. Really close.

So I could smell his...aftershave? Body wash? Soap? Something woodsy. "Of course I'm all right." I might've snapped that.

He blinked—clearly not have expecting that shrewish response. "Look, I don't know you—"

"You're right, you don't." I checked again that we were alone. I'd watched all the kids leave. Well, Kenji had hung around until I'd finally given him the signal to take off.

Johnnie had generously signed autographs for all the kids who wanted one.

George had moved off to the side and pretended to flip through his notebook.

Our guest hadn't appeared to take offense.

When the bell rang, most of the kids blew out of there.

Kenjy, Greta, and Madison were the exceptions.

To my surprise, Johnnie hauled four balls from his bag. He autographed one for each of the kids—and the fourth one to me.

"I'm fine."

"No, you're not. Even I can see you've got a headache."

I scowled.

He rolled his eyes. "Do you want me to tell Louella?"

"Uh...no." My coworker would get in my face about not having taken something. "I took a volleyball to the head. It's not a big deal. Hey."

Damn man moved even closer and gazed into my eyes. His fathomless blue ones stunned in their intensity. Between the gorgeous eyes and the blond hair in a man bun—why did I have to find those so sexy? He was...the whole package. And breathtakingly similar to my ex. Both in looks and temperament.

"Can you take something? Do you need a ride home? Do you have someone at home to take care of you?"

"Steve and Sam will take good care of me."

His eyes widened. "You've got, like, two roommates? Or partners? Sam as in Samuel or Samantha? Or is the person nonbinary and uses Sam as androgynous? Is one a husband or a wife? Are you in one of those triad things? No judgment on my part. And, frankly, none of my business, but that's so cool. I mean, I didn't realize you're gay. Well, if you are gay. Or bi. Not that it matters if you are."

"Johnnie—"

"My teammate Isaiah's gay. And engaged to this awesome guy, Travis. They're getting married once the season's over. Only they have to get married twice—once here and once in New Zealand because that's where most of Isaiah's family lives."

"Johnnie."

"Yes?" He blinked.

"I'm not in a triad relationship."

"Oh, are you just with Sam, and Steve lives with you, or—"

"Steve and Sam are my tabby cats. I didn't name them—although I wouldn't have picked cutesy names anyway. Hey—"

Johnnie had stepped right into my personal space and began palpating the side of my head.

"Fuck, that hurts."

"Yeah, you're developing a goose egg. With your skin color, though, it's hard to see a bruise."

"Best thing about being Black—no one can see me blush." Even as I said the words, heat rose to my cheeks. I could name any number of great things about being Black. I'd thought my husband loved me *despite* being Black. I'd been wrong. He'd loved me *because* I was Black. When I did things that didn't fit his stereotypical view, he'd get annoyed with me. I hadn't seen that during our marriage—I sure as shit saw it clearly now.

"That's true." He continued to gently probe. "Whereas my lily-white ass can be seen reflecting the sun from a million miles away."

My mind very much liked the image of his ass. Color didn't matter—I wasn't picky. Had I noticed his butt in those khaki pants? I'd be lying if I said I hadn't. "I'm really okay."

He held three fingers before me.

"Three. Not blurry or seeing double. Look, I have a hard head—"

"I'd say so."

"What?"

"You don't seem to like me very much."

Ouch. How do I refute that? "Look, I'm incredibly grateful you came today. Louella booked you, so she was disappointed she missed the session." We hadn't actually spoken, obviously, but I knew her heart.

"She was very kind when I called. I kind of booked myself, though. I convinced her I could be helpful."

"Well, you were."

"Really?" He eyed me. "Why do I get the feeling you're lying?"

"I don't lie." *Liar. For years you told everyone you had a great marriage. Note to self—you didn't.*

"Everybody lies."

"Isn't that a song lyric?" I wracked my brain, but stopped when the pain increased. "Look, I need to be heading home."

"No after-school activity?"

"Lacrosse, which Ms. Delmont teaches. She's brilliant, having been a player herself for years. Now she teaches physics and gets out her pent-up energy by coaching. I'm lucky I get a bit of a break."

"So, let me drive you home."

"I've got my SUV—"

"You're not safe to drive."

"I can't leave my car in the parking lot overnight." I didn't have the newest SUV on the market, but I didn't want it...played with. Or removed without my permission.

"Well, my car's a beater. I can leave it here and come back for it later." He held out his hands.

I cocked my head.

"Keys. I'll drive you home and then make my way back here. You don't live in Mission City or Langley or something, do you?" He eyed me.

"Nope." I blew out a breath. "Kensington-Cedar Cottage. Near Trout Lake."

"Nice area." He appeared to consider. "Can't say I spend much time there."

"I managed to get a house. All I could afford after—"

Several long moments passed as those blue eyes assessed me. "After...?"

"My divorce. We, uh, used to live somewhere...more upscale. When he left me, he gave me half of the worth of our house in cash and shooed me out the door. His new...girlfriend...lives with him."

"But he's a dude."

"Yep."

"And you're gay."

"Yep."

"But he's now with a woman."

"Turns out he was bi-curious."

He frowned. "Is that a bad thing?"

"To be bisexual? Absolutely not. To boot out your husband of fifteen years because you met a younger more-attractive woman and you're bored with being married? Possibly."

"Yikes." Johnnie actually winced. "And you still haven't given me your keys. I can totally hop a bus back here to get my car."

"Where do you live?"

"A one-bedroom apartment in Gastown."

"That must make for tight quarters."

"Huh?" His brow knit.

"You and your girlfriend in a one-bedroom."

"How do you know about my girlfriend?" He did not look pleased when I said the blatantly obvious.

"Well, I checked your social media, of course. If you were up to some crazy shit, I would've vetoed the visit to the school. I'm big on protecting my kids as much as possible."

"Oh." He held out his hands.

"I swear I'm fine. I don't even have a headache."

He narrowed his eyes.

Fucking hell. "I was planning to take a painkiller."

"Which you need to do with food. Let's grab Subway or something on way to your place. My treat. Do you have a bag?"

I pursed my lips even as the lacrosse team made their way out of the changing rooms and to the door to the outside.

Louella exited our office with her knapsack. "Everything okay?"

Johnnie's warning was clear. If I didn't do what he wanted, he was going to tattle on me. *What is he? Five?*

"Everything's fine. Johnnie's just going to come by my place."

Louella's eyebrows shot up to her hairline.

"To discuss my next visit." Johnnie gave her the winsomest smile I'd ever seen. All innocent and friendly.

Charming.

"Oh lovely. I wish I could join you. Gotta run." She waved, yanked on her slicker, and headed out into the rain.

I put my keys into Johnnie's hand. "I have to pack my bag and take the painkiller." My head was throbbing.

"Great. I'll pack up my stuff, and we'll be on our way."

He didn't have much to *pack up*, but I didn't comment. Instead, I made my way into the office. I unlocked my desk drawer, dumped two pills into my palm, and downed them with a bit of water from my steel bottle. The water was warm, but I didn't give a shit.

"Ready?" Johnnie leaned against the doorjamb.

I relocked my drawer and grabbed my messenger bag. I unlocked the laptop from the docking station and shoved it into the bag.

"Hey, I hope you're not planning on using that tonight. You need to rest your brain."

"Sheesh." I rolled my eyes.

That hurt my head more.

"Uh, no. But I don't leave it in the office overnight, though." I was about to heft the bag over my shoulder.

He grabbed it.

Short of a tug-of-war, I wasn't going to win. I might have some muscles, but he had an athlete's build with strength to spare. He was also almost a decade younger and a professional rugby player. Not someone to fuck around with.

"I need my keys back to lock the office."

"Fine." He handed them over. "You drive stick?"

"Uh...no." I locked the door and handed him the keys since I wasn't up for another argument. "Why?"

"I love driving stick. My Mazda's a five-speed, and I adore it."

"Here's where I admit I've never driven a manual transmission car." I directed us toward the door. "Never even tried it."

"Oh my God, you're so missing out. I'm going to teach you." He bounced as he walked, clearly thrilled at the prospect of teaching me something.

I almost rolled my eyes—then I remembered how poorly that'd gone the last time. "How about we just make it to my house in one piece?"

"Sure." He offered another charming grin. "I can't wait."

Chapter Four

Johnnie

C oach Yardley's ride was mighty sweet. "2023?"

"2024." He sank into the passenger seat and rested his head against the headrest. "He gave it to me the month before he kicked me out."

"Your ex? Ouch."

"Part of his grand plan. He wanted the courts to see what a generous guy he was."

"Booting you out of the marital home?" I pushed the button, and the electric system purred to life. So damned quiet compared to my car—that had needed a new muffler last decade. Oh well, no one could claim they hadn't heard me coming.

"He considered it an amicable uncoupling. I'm supposed to be grateful because his salary as a podiatrist was always significantly higher than mine as a high—"

"Guy works with feet all day?"

"Uh...yeah. Very rich feet." He pressed a hand to his forehead.

"This thing know where home is?" I gestured to the GPS.

"Yes."

I tapped and regarded the map. "Well, there's a Subway on the way, so we're good. What do you want?"

"Is there any point in arguing?"

"Do you have some moral argument against me buying you a sub? Would you prefer a burger? A salad? A poke bowl?"

He sighed. "A sub is fine."

"Great." I pointed the beautiful SUV toward Somerville Street, with a detour to Subway, and headed out of the parking lot. I cast a look at my fifteen-year-old car, hoped no one touched it, and pulled onto the street. At a red light, I glanced at Coach. "You don't look so good."

He groaned. "I hate taking painkillers."

"Well, yeah." The light turned green, and I advanced. "But having a bad headache is worse. A volleyball, you say? Must've just hit you wrong. Those things are soft."

"Didn't feel soft when it hit my temple." He cracked an eye open, hit a button on the dashboard, and resettled.

I snickered. "Heated seat?"

"You're free to do the same. I don't need comfort like that—but he paid for it, and damn it, I'm going to use it."

"I still can't believe he works with feet. What'd you mean, rich feet?"

"His practice is in Kitsilano. That's where we used to live."

"And he bought your half of the house?" I whistled.

"Turns out he'd been squirreling money away for years. He insisted to the court that he only had enough to buy me out."

I made a right turn onto Broadway. "You didn't believe him?"

"My lawyer didn't. I was too tired to hire someone to go digging. I got enough to buy a nice, little house, and I got away from him. I still have my pension, which after thirty-five years of teaching will look pretty sweet. I put some extra money aside every month—my house is older and needs lots of repairs."

I hung a left on Fraser Street. "Sounds complicated."

"It's my life. Don't think I'm bitter..."

"Much." I grinned because he couldn't see me.

"Much," he conceded. "I got to keep my friends. His...I don't even miss them. Nor do I miss my mother-in-law. She never liked me."

"And you were married for how long?"

"Too long." He let out a sigh.

I pulled into the restaurant parking lot. "Okay, you want to come in?"

"Nope."

"I'm taking the keys so you won't drive away."

"Yep. Wasn't planning on it."

"What do you want?"

"Honestly? Nothing. I'm nauseous."

"All the more reason to get something in your stomach." I wracked my brain. "Meatball? Cold cut?"

"BLT. Extra tomatoes. Oh, with onions and black olives."

"Uh, can you repeat that?"

"Bacon, lettuce, extra tomatoes, onions, black olives, Italian dressing." He sighed. "I might be able to eat that."

Personally, I thought bacon might be a little harsh, and black olives? Blech. "Sure. Back in a few."

That turned out to be overly optimistic as the line was long. I yanked out my phone, pulled up IG, selected my profile, and started scrolling. Me with Carly. Me with my team. Me with Carly. Carly in my place. Me and the guys. Carly and... On it went. Yeah, if Yardley had checked this out, I could see how he assumed Carly and I were...tight.

Even as I was about to put the phone away, she texted asking me where I was.

I responded, *with a friend*, and put the phone in my back pocket.

And ignored the next five texts.

She wasn't great at taking a hint. She was...possessive.

I was...not willing to rock the boat.

After I secured our subs, a couple of cookies, and bottled drinks, I headed back to the SUV.

Yardley barely stirred, so I tossed the food onto the back seat. Within a moment, I was back on the road.

Dodging rush-hour traffic down Fraser Street was a pain, but eventually I found myself before a cute house on Somerville Street. An elevated bungalow painted a bright blue, it fit in with most of the other houses on the street—except a couple where obviously the previous home had been torn down and a much bigger one had replaced it. That happened a lot everywhere in Vancouver. "Do I park out front of—"

"There's a driveway off the back lane." He muttered the words.

"Got it." I figured out how to get there and was grateful he had the number posted on the chain-link fence. I pulled into the driveway and put the SUV into park. After a moment, I turned the vehicle off. "This is a sweet ride."

"You mean aside from the fact the thing was a bribe?" Yardley opened his eyes.

"You're better off without him." I didn't know Dr. What's His Face Podiatrist, MD, but nothing was as bad as being with someone who didn't want you.

"Sure. Maybe." He rubbed his forehead. "Only I was with him for most of my adult life. I didn't know how to live alone. Don't." He corrected himself. "Might as well come in."

"Okay." I grinned. Truthfully, I couldn't figure out if he was perpetually grumpy or if the circumstances were dictating his annoyance. Me? The knock to the head? Discussions about his ex? All? None? Some combination? I had no idea.

I snagged the food as well as my bag. While my attention was focused on that, Yardley snagged his messenger bag with that heavy laptop. "Hey."

"You snooze, you lose." He deadpanned that. Then held out his hand.

I dropped the keys into them as I filled my arms with stuff. By the time I made my way up to his deck, he had the front door unlocked.

"Oh, I have a woman living in the basement. Please don't stomp or be too loud."

"You rent out the basement?" I shucked my shoes.

"Mortgage helper." He paused. "Although I don't have a mortgage. With the housing crunch in this city, I didn't want to leave a perfectly good suite empty. She's a PhD student at UBC. Keeps to herself and is almost never around. I put the rent money aside for a rainy day." He gazed upward. "I'm likely to need a new roof within the next five years."

"Something I don't have to worry about. Do you need help to take your shoes off?"

"I can take off my own shoes, for fuck's sake." Yet, when he tried to bend, he swayed.

"Okay, Coach, let's get you seated. Dining table or couch?" From where we stood, at the back of the house in the kitchen, I spotted the table as well as a very comfortable-looking sectional. "That looks comfy." I gestured with my chin.

"Dirty shoes." He might've whined that.

"I'll mop your floor." I eyed his shoes. They sure didn't look dirty to me. Not like my cleats looked like after a game or practice when the rain poured down and the mud was everywhere.

"You're very argumentative."

I snickered. "Have you listened to yourself lately?" I snagged his messenger bag and placed it gently on the floor. "There for tomorrow. Now—couch, dining table, or bed?"

His eyes went wide. "I didn't say anything about—"

"Nope. But if you're dizzy, then lying down might be a good idea. I'm still not convinced I shouldn't be running you to an after-hours walk-in clinic—"

"I probably would've gotten the headache even if the ball hadn't hit me. The weather." He vaguely pointed out the lovely, large window over the sink. It faced the amazing backyard. Not huge in size, but lush in greenery. I spotted flower plants everywhere. *It'll be amazing when they all bloom.* And he appeared to have a vegetable garden in the back corner. I'd oriented myself, and his backyard faced west and got direct sunlight for most of the day. Perfect for growing.

All of which my mother had taught me before she died.

My uncle, who then took over as my guardian, hadn't had time for *girly shit like that.* To his credit, he'd gotten me interested in rugby. I'd thank the old bastard—if he hadn't died years ago.

I was alone in the world.

You have Carly. You have your teammates. You're not alone, for fuck's sake.

"Couch. Jesus, I'm just tired."

"We'll get you fed and into bed. Are the bedrooms on this floor?"

"Yes, two on this floor as well as two in the attic."

"Nice. Four-bedroom houses are lovely." I didn't know what the fuck I was talking about, but he was letting me guide him to the couch.

I got him plopped onto his butt, and I set about removing his shoes. Actually... "Travis and Isaiah? The couple I told you about? They bought a house in East Van. Up near Sunrise and Hastings. Isaiah's got a massive family back in New Zealand."

I grinned as I got both shoes removed. I headed back to the kitchen. "And his grandmother—who apparently is not to be argued with—has decided various of his nieces and nephews need to come to Canada for various reasons. Mostly schooling, but apparently one kid's, like, a hellion. They figure Uncle Travis will set him straight." I washed my hands, then grabbed two plates from the cupboard. "Travis was in an accident and has a scar down his face and a bunch of tattoos. He comes off as a badass. The truth? He's a softie. If the kids need discipline, Isaiah will take care of that." I plated the subs, then set about getting glasses of ice. "You want lemonade or iced tea? I wasn't certain which you'd want. Unless you have—"

"Lemonade sounds good."

Score. I love iced tea. I'd have drunk the lemonade, of course. "Right. One second." I found a couple of glasses and poured the drinks. "So, I think even if Isaiah's grandmother wasn't sending half of New Zealand, my friends would be looking to foster or even adopt. They're..." I sighed. "You know how some people are meant to be parents? That's them. Although Travis will argue about that continuously. He's getting better, though. Being around Roger's kids has really softened him.

I made my way into the living room with Coach's food and drink.

He had a weird look on his face.

"You okay?"

"Sure. Uh, thanks for the food." He held out his hands.

He's anything but fine. He looks...stricken. I replayed the last few minutes. *Oh God, does he have kids? Did he lose them in a custody dispute?*

Suddenly two balls of fur came careening into the room.

Yardley chuckled as he took the food and drink from me. "I wondered when you two would show up."

"They don't greet you at the door?"

Both fuzzballs leapt onto the couch. One with way more grace than the other.

"The skinny one's Sam, and the fat one's Steve."

"Oh well, I wasn't going to comment on..."

Sam planted himself, opened his legs, and started licking... Yep, he was licking his dick.

Yardley rolled his eyes.

Steve tried to make a grab for the sub.

"Do they need to be fed or something?"

Both cats finally paid some attention to me.

"Oh, did I say the right word? Food?"

"Meow." Steve tumbled off the couch and started headbutting my leg with his nose.

Sam regarded me with solemn eyes.

"He's a little slower to trust." Yardley put his drink on the end table and started petting his cat.

I arched an eyebrow. "Are you going to eat your sub with that hand?"

He snickered. "Not something I generally worry about."

"Gross." I stomped back to the kitchen, Steve hot on my heels. "What do I feed him?"

"Half of one of the containers. Sam can have an entire one and the other half of Steve's."

"Steve won't try to steal?"

"He tried once and got a whack on the nose for his trouble. Sam takes his food very seriously."

I gazed down to find both cats staring up at me. "In these little dishes?"

"Yes, that's perfect."

"Well, okay, then." I muttered the words under my breath. Within moments, I was directing each cat to a dish. I probably didn't need to supervise—given Sam knew how to put Steve in his place—but I figured sticking around would be good.

Except—

I grabbed a paper towel, wet it, and headed into the living room.

Coach had his sub in both hands and was devouring it.

"Gross. Seriously." I stalked over to him. "Didn't your mother teach you any manners?"

"Didn't have a mother." He glared. But he took the wet towel and wiped his hands.

"Oh, I'm sorry."

"I'm not. According to my dad, she wasn't all that nice of a woman. She gave birth to me, stuck around for a little while, then met someone else and took off. Left my dad with me and my older sister."

"You're a younger child? I had you pegged as the eldest."

He glared.

I snickered, snagged the dirty towel from his hand, and went back to the kitchen. I tossed it, washed my hands, then headed back into the living room with my sub and iced tea.

He was nearly finished while I hadn't even started. I put my glass down on the end table and plopped next to him with a sigh.

"You're..." He eyed me. "Bossy."

I laughed. "You're the coach and you're calling me bossy? I might be the captain of the team, but everyone listens to Roger since he's older and has been around longer."

"Roger who's got kids?"

Funny how that fact had stuck with him. "Five. Kristine Angelique's just a couple of months old. Cassandra's twelve, Tristan's almost nine, Linus is six, and Evelyn's three, and you should be damn impressed I remembered all that." In fact, I hadn't always been so diligent about keeping track of my teammates' kids. Then Isaiah joined the squad, and by the third day, he knew everyone and all their offspring. Not to be outdone, I tried to keep up as well.

I settled in to eat my sub, all the while wondering what the fuck I was doing here.

Chapter Five

Yardley

*H*e's the first man you've had in here other than your friends, and *he's...straight.* Not that my friends didn't count. They were just...all paired up. *Maybe you can call Johnnie a friend. Then your streak remains unbroken.*

Right. Like that was somehow the most important thing going on at this moment. I sipped my lemonade—which happened to be my favorite drink. I should've offered him first pick, since he was the guest, but I was *not* an iced tea fan. At all. Lemonade, though, was a treat I never turned down.

As Louella and Hugo both knew. If they brought me one, they were usually trying to bribe me.

Johnnie moaned as he finished his meatball sub. Obviously a favorite and probably why he'd suggested it.

I enjoyed them, but would've likely found it too heavy. Bacon grease never upset my stomach, so the BLT had been a good choice. "Thank you."

"You're welcome." He grinned that oh-so-perfect grin. "How's your head?"

I took stock. "Still hurts, but not as much as before. No dizziness and, now I've eaten, no nausea. So, I guess you can go home now. Do you want me to drive you to your car?"

He scowled. "The entire point of driving you home was so that you wouldn't be behind the wheel. *Still hurts* isn't *all gone and I'm perfect, thanks*. Even then, I wouldn't allow you back behind—"

"Allow? No one allows me to do anything. I'm a grown adult. No matter what Jamilla tells you—"

"Who's Jamilla?"

"My older sister. What I'm trying to say—"

"Is she single?"

"That no one bosses..." I squinted. "What?"

"I'm just wondering if your sister's single."

"Okay. I'm almost afraid to ask why you want to know. That's an incredibly personal question—"

"You said she was older. So, I'm wondering if she has other people in her life, or if she's dedicated to bossing you around. You don't seem like the type to just sit back and be ordered around."

I blinked. Because he sort of had my relationship with Jamilla nailed. "She's married with three kids. Her husband's name is Reuben and, smart man, he sits back and lets her run the show."

"Three kids?"

My heart panged. "Three nephews. All chaos agents, despite their military-style upbringing by their mother. Kolson leads the crew at a grown-up sixteen. Then Roland is thirteen. Meyer brings up the rear at four." I smiled as I thought fondly about my nephews. "She really wants a girl, but she had three miscarriages before getting pregnant with Meyer. For everyone involved, they've decided three's a good number."

"They could always adopt."

I cocked my head. "That's true. I mean they're a solid middle-class family with a nice home and could offer a ton of love." I swallowed. "They're good, though."

"Any athletes in the making?"

"Uh, well..." I hesitated.

He arched an eyebrow. "That was a pretty easy question—unless they're all math geeks in the making and completely uncoordinated."

"Well, that's not a thing. Meyer's too young to have picked a sport, but he's a devil on skates. Roland loves throwing and really wants to be a quarterback."

"Ah." He waited. For a very long time. "And Kolson?"

"Oh." I examined my fingernails.

"Is there something wrong—"

"He wants to be a rugby player."

"Ah." Johnnie eyed me. "And you think I'd be a bad influence on him."

"That's a hell of a stretch."

He arched an eyebrow.

"Okay." I rubbed my face, wincing at the pain elicited by the added pressure. "I told you—I looked at your socials. As well as your teammates'. You think I wouldn't prefer Roger or Isaiah as a potential role model?"

"Isaiah's gay."

"So am I. And the kids know it. I don't give two shits about someone's sexuality—and neither do Jamilla and Reuben. But they want their kids following the straight and narrow. Doesn't do a Black boy any good to get in trouble. I mean, you don't want any kids being truant or getting involved in illegal activity. But that's even more for racialized kids. Our police force might slowly—and I mean slowly—be becoming more colorful. But there's still a ton of prejudice out there. I'm sure you know the statistics." Except maybe that was arrogance on my part. I lived the reality of being a Black man in Canada. Better than the States, for sure, but still a huge challenge. I didn't want my nephews to face discrimination. I wanted them to have all the same opportunities as their white classmates. To never be seen as *less than* because of the color of their skin.

"I might not know the exact statistics, or the lived experience of Black kids, but one of my former teammates, Bruce, gets pulled over by the cops repeatedly. Yet, I've never been. Nor have Roger or Jason. We all knew the reason and railed against the injustice of it." He sighed. "But I don't see why you think I'd be such a bad influence. I'm kind of hurt. I don't drink to excess. I don't womanize."

I started to speak.

He cut me off. "I'm always monogamous. Yes, there have been a few women—but never more than one at a time. I have a bit of a reputation, partly because of my looks, but I'm just an ordinary guy."

Because of my looks.

Ha.

The man was fucking sex on a stick. Gorgeous. I didn't doubt he had women falling at his feet. I wanted to believe those women wanted more than just a good-looking man on their arms.

Hell, he probably had men falling at his feet as well.

Still, all I managed to do was yawn.

He grinned. "I'm boring you? All this professing that I'm just an ordinary guy?"

I sighed. "If I tell Kolson that I've met you, he's going to be stoked. He's going to want to meet you."

"And you think that will be a problem? Tell you what..." He tilted his head. "I was planning to offer a clinic to Greta, Kenji, and any other kid in the school who wants to come. Would it be weird if Kolson attended? I was going to ask Isaiah and Jason to come. Roger, too, if he's up for it. He's pretty busy with the newborn."

"You'd do that? Run a clinic for the kids?" That was way more than just dropping by and shooting the shit with the kids like he had today. "There are some younger kids who would definitely come and yeah, I can make certain staff know they can invite their kids. Then it won't be weird if Kolson comes." No one would question if my nephew showed up anyway—he'd dropped by a few times over the years. "Seriously, though? You're not just saying this?"

"To what end? What would I get from lying to you and promising something I don't intend to deliver? That just ruins my reputation as a good guy."

I almost suggested he was being nice to get into my pants.

Yeah, suggesting that to the straight guy, even as a joke, probably won't go over well. And I couldn't suggest he was interested in my sister either—which had been my first flash thought when he brought her up. "If you're serious, I can make it happen. You think your guys will be interested in coming?"

"Isaiah teaches high school, so he's definitely interested. He's just in his first year, though, so he's still feeling his way around."

God, I remembered what those days were like.

"That's why I would suggest after school or on a Saturday. Then he can come, and he might bring a couple of kids as well."

"Did you have all this planned, or are you—"

"Winging it? Totally winging it." He put his plate on the coffee table and yanked out his phone. "How's next Monday afternoon? If we do it after school, I suspect Isaiah could make it. I can text him if you're good."

"I can't speak for my students—lots have part-time jobs—but if I announce it tomorrow, I suspect most will be able to make the time."

"Great." He grinned, but continued typing on his phone.

Within moments of him ceasing, it buzzed like, six times.

"Okay. Jason, Isaiah—and even Roger—are in."

"That's fantastic. I'll put an announcement out tomorrow and let all the kids know. Isaiah will tell his students?"

"Yep. He teaches just down the road from you, and I'm certain he'll have kids who will hop the bus and head your way. Friendly rivalry, right?"

"Oh, yeah. I know which school you're talking about. They beat us at football and we always kick their asses on the basketball court." I winced. "Our football equipment isn't quite as good as theirs. Not a reason for losing, but it doesn't help either."

"You don't do, like, fundraisers and stuff?"

"Who are we trying to fundraise from? Our kids come from lower-income homes. We apply for grants and stuff, but there's only so much money to go around. That's why rugby's such a great sport. Sure, there's a bit of equipment—but not gear like football. Rugby's an equal-opportunity sport."

He grinned. "You get it. I mean, my uncle had money, so I could've played whatever I wanted. Except he was a 15s fan. England, to be specific. He felt Canada should never have become an independent country."

I blinked. "Seriously?"

"Yeah. He was deferential to Queen Elizabeth, but he really wanted a king back on the throne."

"That's..."

"Sexist? Misogynist? You better believe it. Every day, I heard how useless women were." His eyes shadowed. "I'd like to think I'm better than him."

I closed my left eye, trying to understand his words. "You think you're like him? Disrespecting women?"

"No." His phone buzzed again. He glanced down and winced. "Sorry, I really need to make a phone call."

"Not a problem. I need to clean up. Do you want me to call you a cab?"

"I was wondering if I might crash here tonight? I'm worried about your head."

"Uh, unless you suddenly don't have a home, you're not staying here. My head's fine, thank you. A couple more painkillers before bed, and I'll be perfect by tomorrow."

He looked doubtful.

I pointed to his phone.

Again, he winced. "Yeah, can't put this off." Sounded like something he definitely didn't want to do. "I'll call a cab myself. Thanks for dinner." He headed to the kitchen.

Before I was even able to rise, he was gone.

I sat, a little stunned.

He thanked *me* for dinner? He'd paid for it. Had put it on plates—which was way more than I would've done. He'd been a true gentleman with me. Taking better care of me than most people I knew. Certainly more than Nicholas ever would have. The time I'd caught a norovirus and had been so sick I'd thought I'd have to go to the hospital? He'd kicked me out of our bedroom and sequestered me in a guest bedroom. He'd brought fancy soup that made me sicker and complained when I hadn't been able to attend an awards banquet with him.

I'd felt guilty.

In retrospect, I was sorry I hadn't given him the damn bug.

A week later, and seven pounds lighter, I'd emerged. With a new-found respect for nurses who cared for people like myself. I'd never been that sick in my life.

The back door shut.

Slowly, I eased forward on the couch. *If he wanted to stay, he totally could have. You have three guest bedrooms.* Two were in an attic space where he would've had to duck, but he probably could've managed.

I took the plates to the kitchen, then returned for the glasses. I poured the bit of Johnnie's iced tea that remained down the sink and chugged my lemonade. As I stood over the sink, I took stock. My head had a dull ache, but nothing bad. I certainly didn't have a concussion or lasting damage. As Johnnie said—volleyballs were softer than other balls.

After putting the dishes in the dishwasher, I had a quick shower, donned my pajamas, hopped into bed to read for a bit, and tried not to think about the enigma that was Johnnie Leclerc.

Chapter Six

Johnnie

"It's really great you're willing to do this." My gaze moved between Isaiah, Roger, Jason, as well as Francine who'd tagged along.

She grinned. "I'll take them through a few exercises and then just sit back and watch. No bleachers, eh?" She glanced around the field.

"At least they have a field." Isaiah winced. "That's not always a given."

In poverty-stricken areas like this one. He didn't have to say the words—we all understood them.

"Hey, sorry I'm late." Raheem, our right wing, sauntered over. "Anyone else have problems with parking?" His dark, tight, curly hair was a little on the frizzy side today, despite the sun.

Everyone's hand shot up.

"Me, too." Makwa joined us. He was one of the best outside centers in the league.

Finally, Irvin strode over. "I took the bus. But there was an accident on Hastings Street, and so I got jammed up. I hopped off and ran here." Yet the man had hardly broken a sweat. He dropped his bag on the ground. "Okay, let's do this." The loosehead prop was always down for anything.

I swallowed. "I can't believe you all came out today."

Isaiah slapped me on the back. "You think we were going to leave the teaching up to you? The next generation of players will be *so* confused."

Everyone chuckled.

I was so grateful, I couldn't find it within myself to be annoyed. I knew this game as well as anyone on the team. My uncle ensured that.

The door to the gym opened and, with Yardley in the lead, about fifteen kids emerged.

Louella brought up the rear.

"Oh, is she taken?" Makwa's eyes widened. His tan skin contrasted with his white jersey.

"Even if she's single, now's not the time." Roger glared.

"Never harm in looking, right, Johnnie?"

Since my eyes were on Yardley, I couldn't exactly scold him. I slapped him on the back. "The kids are the focus, okay? And she's got a wedding ring."

He appeared crestfallen, but it was all an act. Although I had the playboy reputation, Makwa did quite well with the ladies. To the point I wondered if he would ever settle down.

I grinned when Yardley approached. "These are my mates."

Jason pointed to himself. "I use the term. As you can tell from my accent, I'm not from around here."

"And where are you from?" Louella managed to herd the kids into a semicircle, with her on one end and Yardley on the other—closest to me.

"England. Liverpool, in particular. So, everyone asks me why I don't play football. Oh, soccer."

A few of us laughed.

Some of the kids appeared confused.

"To be difficult, the rest of the world calls soccer football while North Americans call it soccer and refer to football as football." Yardley frowned. "Well, football with all the gear and the brown-leather ball."

"That's a little nuts." Kenji grinned. "Which is why I love rugby."

Jason pumped his fist. "Awesome."

"Let's go around the circle and introduce ourselves. If you have a position, share it. No worries if you don't, okay?" Yardley surveyed the group.

I eyed him. *I wonder what position he plays?* Which sounded way dirtier in my head than I intended it to be.

About half the students had favorite positions and the others didn't. Quickly, I could see we had a good mix of body sizes, strengths, and potential vulnerabilities. I was also thrilled Greta had brought two friends from another school—Sophie and Hope.

Francine took us through stretches to get started.

Makwa kept an eye on Louella, and she seemed to be keeping an eye on him. Her wedding ring seemed to have disappeared since last Monday, but that didn't mean anything—she might not normally wear it to school. Still, the two were worth keeping an eye on.

As was Yardley. In deference to the warm March day, most of the teens wore shorts and T-shirts. As a surprise, I'd brought twenty Orcas jerseys. Yardley knew, as he'd helped me figure out sizes. Bringing a couple of extras just in case felt like a good idea.

"Now, you're warmed up, Roger's going to take you through some basic skills you're going to need." Francine grinned. "Pay attention. He might not be the captain, but he's got the most experience. When he tells you to do something, you'd better listen."

"Coach always overrides Roger, though." I grinned. "Coach Lawrence is a beast if he's mad at you."

"Coach Morrison's the best." Tatum, who wasn't even that much into rugby, had shown up. Helped us put together a team, so I was grateful.

"You're already getting an A." Louella grinned. "But a little sucking up never hurt."

"On that note, we're going to go through different ways of passing. Remember, it's always to the side." Roger nabbed a couple of balls.

"But we're going to practice scrum, right?" Kolson, Yardley's nephew held up his hand. "That's where I'm weakest."

"We can absolutely practice scrum." Roger eyed his teammates. "While Johnnie runs you through the plays, I'll divvy us up into teams. No roughhousing though, okay? This is just for fun."

Kolson didn't look thrilled, but Kenji slapped him on the back. "We can get together and practice, okay?"

Yardley appeared startled at first, likely because the boys were from different high schools and clearly different social strata. Kolson's cleats were easily five times the cost of Kenji's shoes.

"That would be great. I want to make the Orcas when I graduate." Kolson eyed me.

"Entirely possible. Let's see what you've got." I tipped my chin toward Roger.

"Since I'm older, I'll be on the team by then." Kenji beamed.

Three hours later, I didn't have any doubts. Damn kid was amazing. Every single pass he made, he nailed. Same with the kicks.

Kolson was hot on his heels, though. Greta, Sophie, and Hope were all clearly talented, and I was left in no doubt why they were on a local team.

Some of the other kids struggled a bit. More than a few fumbled balls. Some confusion as to what to do when they caught one.

All that said, I could honestly say each kid's skills had improved at the end of the session, and each of my teammates beamed with pride as they handed out the jerseys. We'd split the cost between the seven of us, which helped a lot. Professional rugby players in Canada didn't make much money—hence us all having to supplement our incomes with side gigs.

As the kids were dispersing, a stunning Black woman approached the group. She wore burgundy leather boots, a dark-blue wool skirt, and an expensive wool coat. She high-fived Kolson, so I made the leap this was Yardley's sister, Jamilla.

And ouch, she wasn't just older. Even without the heels on the boots, she was a couple of inches taller than her brother.

"Mom, I want you to meet Johnnie." Kolson encouraged her to move toward me.

I managed a wave.

She pushed her black, curly hair from her face. "So, you're the famous Johnnie."

I cocked my head.

"Oh, Yardley's been talking about you—how this was all your idea. Moreover, Kolson wants a spot on your squad. I think he's aiming for yours." She grinned.

"Hooker, eh?" I grinned. Kolson had already mentioned that. He certainly had the build for it. Even at sixteen, he had some bulk.

And decent height—which he clearly got from his mother, although perhaps his father was tall as well.

"Hey, Jamilla." Yardley pressed a kiss to her cheek. "Glad you could make it."

"To see my baby get beat up? I'll always make the time." She caught my gaze. "Divorce attorney. One of the best in Vancouver." She grinned. "I'm looking at buying my rival's practice. Silly man wants to move to a small-town and take it easy." She rolled her eyes.

Kolson groaned.

I chuckled. "Well, I've never gotten married, so I don't have to worry about needing your services."

"Well, if you ever do, I give discounts to Yardley's friends."

Yardley's friend. What exactly had he said about me?

Her smile continued. "Why don't you come to dinner tomorrow night? You can talk Kolson out of playing."

I started to open my mouth.

"Just kidding. You should see the look on your face. Priceless." She touched her son's shoulder. "If this is the path he's set on, far be it from me to dissuade him. I might be a protective mama bear, but I want my kids to be happy."

"Can we invite Kenji too?" Kolson's eyes lit with excitement.

"Sure."

"Great." He pressed a kiss to his mom's cheek, then shouted, "Hey, Kenji! Wait up!"

His affection toward his mother was heartening. His volume left my ears ringing.

"I guess I'd better show up." I laughed ruefully.

She eyed me with a way-too-knowing look. "You're a good guy, Johnnie. I'll thank you in advance and warn you about being railroaded by Morrisons. I might be a Smith, now—and oh God, isn't that just the most boring last name ever—but I'll always be Yardley's big sister at heart. Later." She waved as she headed over to where Kenji, Kolson, and Isaiah stood.

"Isaiah would be a much-better choice for dinner—especially since Kenji wants to be a fullback." Not that I didn't want to go. Kolson had expressed an interest in being a hooker, but, of course, all that might change as he matured and he tried positions that might better fit his body type and abilities.

"My sister's taken a shining to you." Yardley cocked his head. "She knows you organized today, and this is her way of paying you back." Then he muttered, "At least I hope those are her intentions."

"What?"

"Nothing. Do you want me to drive you tomorrow night? Kerrisdale's a bit out of your way."

I squinted. "How is coming from Kensington to Gastown and then back out to Kerrisdale *on* your way? That's a massive triangle. Your house to your sister's is almost a straight shot. How's the head? I forgot to ask."

"Better by the next morning. As Jamilla would say, I've got a hard noggin."

"Just give me her address, and I'll make it there myself. My car might look out of place in that neighborhood, but I'll survive." I chuckled.

"How about I text it to you?" Yardley tapped a code into his phone, tapped a couple more times, and handed me the phone.

I entered my number, sent myself a text, and then completed the new contact sequence. Finally, I handed the phone back with my shit-eating grin.

Yardley arched an eyebrow. "Handsome Johnnie?"

"You don't think I'm gorgeous?" I angled my head to give him my best side.

"Oh God." He pocketed his phone. "See you tomorrow."

I watched as he walked away, feeling like something had shifted in me, but not understanding what.

Isaiah smacked me on the back. "Travis is home and cooking dinner. I know we're in the opposite—"

"I'm not turning down a home-cooked meal." I gave my friend a rueful grin. "Have you heard?"

"That you're having dinner with two prospective players, one teacher, and his sister? Better you than me."

Except he would've been a better choice.

Still, I'd put on my nicest clothes and do my best to put on a good show.

Chapter Seven

Yardley

J ohnnie was more relaxed than I expected he might be.

Maybe I wasn't giving him enough credit.

Perhaps because I was the one who was nervous. With Johnnie's reputation as a ladies' man, along with pro athletes and their loose tongues—I was thinking vulgarity in particular—I expected a bit more of a shitshow.

Instead, he was well-mannered. He paid plenty of attention to Kenji and Kolson, while ensuring Roland and Meyer weren't left out, even though their chosen sports weren't rugby.

Reuben surveyed his kids with papa pride while Jamilla fussed a little more than usual.

After a delicious dinner, Johnnie and I cleared the table—after a battle with the Smith family. My sister ran a tight ship, and everyone was expected to help. Still, Kolson and Kenji heated the brownies and added the vanilla ice cream with varying degrees of success.

Whatever. It all went down the same way, and when Johnnie moaned his pleasure, my cock sat up and paid attention.

Damn thing.

I would've run Kenji home, but his mom came to pick him up after her shift at the hospital, which wasn't far away. She worked as a dietician and although she made a decent salary, Vancouver was damn expensive—especially for a single mom with two growing boys. Which explained why she lived in Strathcona and still struggled.

After waving Kenji and his mom off, Johnnie and I said our good-byes to the Smiths and headed to our respective vehicles.

The night air was crisp, and although we had a full moon, the meteorologist promised rain for the next few days—including for his game Friday night.

"I have something for you." He gave me his wicked grin.

"Oh?" I tried to effectuate disinterest, but the truth was, he intrigued me more and more. Gone was my assumption he was all fluff and no substance. The clinic last night and dinner tonight had solidified that he could, given the right circumstances, be an upright-and-serious guy.

He handed me a ticket. "Next time I'll get some for your entire family. I've just got one for Friday's game."

"That's, uh..." I considered. "Are there still tickets for the game?"

"Yeah, pretty sure."

"Then I'll arrange for tickets for anyone in that insane household who wants to go. And if Kolson wants to invite Kenji, I'll see if Jamilla can buy the ticket."

"Because he's your student?"

"Right. I can't give him a gift or show favoritism. But if Jamilla takes him under her wing, as she clearly wants to do, then that would be okay. I just have to make certain she doesn't go overboard. We didn't have a lot of money growing up. Now she's making big bucks, she wants to give back in every way she can. I have to make certain she doesn't see Kenji as a *project*."

"Good thinking. I can certainly keep an eye on them. Truthfully? They're talented. Almost as much as Greta, Sophie, and Hope. I can see those three competing for spots on the national team when they're old enough." His expression sobered. "Thank you for letting me come to spend time with them. To enable me to get back to my roots."

"Uh, well, Louella agreed."

"You know she and Makwa are on a date tonight, right?"

My jaw dropped. "No, she did not mention that."

"Oops? I didn't mean to step in it."

"Louella's a widow. Her husband died in a bad wreck on the highway about a year back. She puts on a brave face, but she's been grieving." But she had, after Johnnie's visit last week, stopped wearing her wedding ring.

"I didn't know that. Do you suppose she's told Makwa? Should I tell him?"

If I asked him to, then Johnnie would. But... "She's a grown woman who can make her own decisions. Makwa's about as much of a player as you are."

Slowly, he nodded. "We're both monogamous, though. Neither of us have cheated on a partner. I'll...have a chat with him."

I felt badly about interfering, but I really didn't want Louella to get hurt. "I'd appreciate that."

"And I'll ask him to keep the two of us out of it."

"I'd be even more grateful for that."

"In exchange for that, I'd like to ask you something."

Oh dear. I couldn't even imagine what this guy might come up with. "Yes?" That came out with a croak. I cleared my throat. "Sure, anything."

"You might regret that."

"I would say that's a guarantee, but go ahead."

"This is a personal question."

"About me being gay?"

"How did you know?"

"You just have this particular look on your face. Go on, ask the question. It's about me teaching young boys, right?" I'd been waiting for this conversation—it happened frequently.

"No. Not like you think." He shifted from foot to foot. "I don't mean I think there's anything wrong with you teaching kids—but I was wondering how the parents are with you?"

"Yeah—I get some comments, but it's mostly okay. I'm careful not to show too much attention to anyone's kid. To not be alone with them. But that's stuff every teacher does—whether they're gay or not. Accusations are a serious thing. Usually there's some valid reason for them...but sometimes not." I paused. "It was better when I could say I was married. But I got divorced last year, and I'm now atrociously single. Some parents think this means I must be looking at their sixteen-year-olds."

Johnnie laughed. "As if."

"Right. Why look at pimply sixteen-year-olds when I can look at rugged-and-handsome rugby players?"

"Yeah, right." He laughed, but it felt a little forced.

"Don't worry. I know you're dating that model. Carly? I looked you up."

"You did?" He appeared surprised.

Have we not already had this conversation? Maybe he forgot. Maybe it didn't mean as much to him as it meant to me.

"Absolutely. I needed to make sure you weren't going to hit on my pimply sixteen-year-old students."

"Yeah. Don't believe everything you see on social media." Another laugh, this one a touch more genuine.

"You mean you're *not* dating her?" *What's he trying to say? That his feed isn't a reflection of him?*

"I am. Sort of. Maybe. I'll let you know in a week." He tipped his chin up, almost as if daring me to question him further.

Which I wasn't going to do. "A week? You're planning on talking to me in a week? I don't understand."

"Me neither." He gave me a jaunty wave. "So, see you around." He slid into his car, started the engine, then rolled down the window.

All as I continued to stand there, still a little confused.

"Hey!"

"Yeah?"

"You were on my Insta? So you liked that picture of me beside the pool?"

Oh yeah. I remember that one. I laughed. "Of course. Spent a long time staring at it. Would've been better if you'd dropped the towel."

He winked, then drove away.

What the fuck was that all about? If he was gay, I might've thought we were flirting. But he was straight, dating Carly, and had no interest in me in *that* way.

I slid into my SUV and made my way along 41st Avenue until I was back in my neighborhood. As I pulled into my driveway, I sighed. *I own this house. I'm better off without fucking Nicholas and his cheating ass.* Yes, I wasn't living in luxury anymore—comparing Jamilla's house to mine put that into sharp focus. But we were both doing better than our father ever had. We had homes, jobs, and...

Yeah.

Jamilla had the family I always wanted.

I sighed, grabbed my laptop case from where I'd hidden it under my front seat, and headed inside.

Instead of sitting down to work—report cards were due soon—I showered, crawled into bed, and grabbed my phone.

Of course, I headed right to Instagram.

Johnnie's profile, no less.

Because compulsions were a thing.

I'm just making certain there isn't anything untoward. He's mentoring Kolson and Kenji...I need to be careful. Oh, he's posted a new photo.

I squinted.

A picture of a white towel carelessly dropped on the tiles.

Going swimming...

Well, shit.

Chapter Eight

Johnnie

"Holy fuck, I can't believe we got that over the line!" Roger pulled me into a massive hug.

Isaiah tackled me from behind.

Makwa tried to give me a high-five.

The crowd roared their approval. Somehow, despite being down from the get-go, we'd squeaked out a win over Calgary—by three points.

Their team appeared absolutely dejected. I couldn't blame them—they'd come within one play of winning. Which would've broken their eight-game losing streak. Part of me felt sorry for them, the rest was elated.

"Johnnie, you're the best baby!"

Isaiah coughed. "Was that best, baby or best baby?"

I squinted as we lined up to shake the opposing team's hands. "Either sounds bad, don't you think?"

"Is she sitting next to Yardley?"

I winced. "I hadn't thought that through when I gave him the ticket. I should've swapped it. Or..." I cleared my throat.

"Or...?" Isaiah held my gaze.

"Break up with her...?"

"Is that a question or a statement? Only you can decide. You've been dating her for a long time. Aside from Anwa, this is the longest relationship you've had."

Mention of my ex-girlfriend twisted my gut.

"Shit." Isaiah winced as we headed to the locker room. "I shouldn't have said that."

"It's true." I tried to shrug it off.

He cocked his head.

"Nothing. It's nothing." I yanked my shirt over my head. "I need to shower."

"Because Carly's waiting for you, or because Yardley is?"

I scowled. "Yardley's sister, her entire family, and Kenji are out there. Yardley will leave with them."

"Are you certain?"

"Of course." But I wasn't, so I hustled through my shower. Then I donned my nice jeans, a henley that matched my eyes—or so Roger's wife Becca assured me—and hustled my way to the meeting area. Surprisingly, I was the first player there. Possibly because after brushing my hair to get the tangles out, then putting it in a man bun in a heartbeat, and then busting my butt.

To find Carly and Yardley off to one side.

Talking.

Shit.

"Uh, hey." I did a little wave.

Carly launched herself at me—wrapping her legs around my waist and placing a kiss to my lips.

I tried to respond. I did. Because she was my girlfriend, and I owed her that much. As I thought about all the other women in my life—like Becca and now Jamilla—I couldn't help thinking how vacuous Carly was. I hadn't seen it before. At least not in such stark contrast against the intelligent, caring, and kind man who stood off to the side, awkwardly watching the spectacle Carly initiated.

Gently, I untangled her from me and set her on the ground. "I need to say *hi* to my friend."

She pouted, with her bright, shiny lips stuck out. Her blonde hair hung loose around her face, and I remembered, for an instant—as I gazed into her luminous light-brown eyes—why I'd found her so attractive in the first place. *Should've looked beyond the surface...you might've seen the truth sooner.* "He's a good guy."

"He's boring."

I winced. Yeah, not a good idea to have put them together. "He's a teacher, Carly. That's an important job."

"I have an important job."

Inwardly, I sighed. "Of course you do. Now, I'll be five minutes."

Her eyes flashed triumph that she'd won my clear attention over the *boring* guy.

I extricated myself and headed over to Yardley.

Some of the other guys joined the crowd, and I heard plenty of cheers.

I leaned in closer to Yardley. "Thank you for coming."

"I'm a coach—I'll always watch a game." He held my gaze. "But that tackle—"

"My knee's fine. Francine checked it out at halftime." Because I'd injured it last year, and she was always worried about a recurrence.

Frankly, so was I. I didn't want to think about injuring myself again and having to sit out more games.

"I'm relieved to hear that. Look, Jamilla, Reuben, and all the kids are headed to White Spot. Not exactly your speed…"

Because I either went home with Carly or went out with the guys for a drink. At the moment, either the guys or Jamilla's crew sounded far better than Carly—but I owed this to her. "Another time, okay? I appreciate that you took care of the tickets for them tonight. Let me see if I can get some for the next game—it's a big one, so we might be sold out."

"We can always watch from Jamilla's media room." He gestured to his slicker. "How she keeps her hair so perfect is beyond me." He gazed over at Carly who stood apart, appearing truly annoyed.

That was unusual for her—usually she was in the middle of everyone, trying to ingratiate herself with my *attractive* teammates.

Vacuous.

In that moment, I hated myself.

I held out my hand. "Uh, thanks so much for coming."

"Nice to see you again. I'll give Jamilla your regrets."

"You have no idea how much I wish I could go."

He held me captive in the depths of his dark-brown eyes.

Wait…what? Why was I wanting to go home with him instead? Like…to a bed or something. *I'm straight. Right? I think I would know if I wasn't.* And yet, the compulsion to caress his face and to apologize again came to me in a rush.

"We'll see you another time." He cleared his throat. "Wouldn't want to disappoint Kenji and Kolson. They've started quite the bromance."

"Fair enough."

"Johnnie." Carly wrapped herself around my side and whispered into my ear, "Take me home and fuck me."

As had happened the last few times she'd done this, my cock didn't respond like it used to. She apparently didn't notice as she nipped my earlobe.

Yardley held my gaze for one more moment before sauntering away.

"Sure. Did you bring your car?"

"Nope. Took the bus. So we can go back to your place, and I'll just have to stay the night."

Nice try. You live on an all-night bus route, and I'm going to be driving you home anyway.

Three hours later, after an epic fight that did *not* lead to epic make-up sex, Carly stormed off and into a cab with a hundred bucks cash from me and a bag of all the stuff she'd *accidentally* left at my place.

It still took me an hour to de-Carly my apartment, small as it was. In the end, I had the place the cleanest it'd been since I moved in and a little box of knickknacks and other weird things she'd somehow infiltrated my home with, to go to the charity shop. Six months was a long time.

I opened my junk drawer and pulled out the photo envelope from the bottom.

Carly had never dug that far down, thank God. I didn't think I could've explained it to her in a way she understood.

In a way I understood.

I sent a text.

Twenty minutes later, I sat in a booth at Jumpin' Jacks across from Yardley. "Thanks for coming."

He rubbed his face. "I'll admit it's pretty late, but that text had me getting dressed and heading here."

"You were undressed? It's Friday night."

"Well, I had a long day. Remember, I'm up pretty damn early. We have archery practice Friday before school."

"Archery?" I squinted. "Really?"

"I have a young woman in a wheelchair. She's got real potential, so I started a club. Most of the other kids are there to keep her company while she kicks ass. I've arranged for her to work with a professional club, and I'm trying to find her a sponsor. I'd love to see her at the Paralympics one day—she's got the talent."

"Okay...wow."

"Yeah, who'd have thought from the poorest school in the region?"

"Kenji might make it to our squad. Surely there've been other kids."

"There have. Which is why I stay and work my ass off. Sometimes sports is a way out of poverty for these kids. A way to get post-secondary education."

"Scholarships?"

"Yep. I encourage dreams whenever I can, and if the kid's got grit, but no potential, I use their interest as a cudgel to get them to study harder."

"Cudgel, eh?"

"Whatever works." He eyed me. "But you didn't text me to hear about archery students."

I rubbed the back of my neck as I eyed my whisky. "I broke up with Carly."

"I want to say I'm sorry. Or that I didn't see it coming. After spending an entire match with her, though..." He blew out a breath. "Although she spent a good chunk of it ignoring me, which was fine. I just..."

"She's..."

"Yeah..."

"And I'm not..."

He cocked his head. "No, you're not. I might've thought you were before, but you've proven you're not...like her."

"While I waited for you, I went through and deleted a ton of my Insta posts. I don't want to be seen as *that guy*."

"I'm proud of you. You're so much more than you portray yourself as. I think you could do some real good in the world—when you're not busy winning matches and cycling around as a courier downtown."

"Near miss yesterday."

"Ouch."

"Pays the bills." I held his gaze. "I want to tell you about something. I don't talk to anyone about this, but I want to talk to you."

"Of course." He was quick to speak. "You can talk to me about anything."

Slowly, I withdrew the worn photo envelope from my pocket and handed it over.

And held my breath.

He withdrew a little strip of black-and-white images. His gaze flew to mine. "Carly?"

"What? Oh God, no." Panic seized me. "No, Carly's not pregnant." *Thank Christ.*

Yardley continued to hold the photos—so damn gently. "I've seen four of these. One for each of Jamilla's boys, of course. And one of the girl who..." He blinked. "She didn't have a properly formed brain and wouldn't have lived. That termination..." He blinked again. "That nearly broke Jamilla. Hell, Reuben and I were right there in the suffering. But she found the courage to do what she had to do. Two more first-trimester miscarriages, and then she had Meyer. My sister..." He blew out a breath. "She's got so much fucking love to give. They're good with their three now, I think. Well, Reuben's been snipped."

I winced. Even as I continued to fixate over huge hands gently holding the picture of my daughter. "Anwa miscarried a month after that ultrasound."

"Aw, shit."

"The pregnancy was an accident. She was on the pill and was diligent about it. Best she figured, the antibiotics she took for a bout of strep throat might've made them less effective. Anyway, she got pregnant, and I planned on marrying her."

"Oh." Yardley's gaze shot to mine. "You loved her?"

"Sure."

He arched an eyebrow. "Not everyone who's pregnant has to get married."

"My baby. No way was she going to be raised in a single-parent household. I cared for Anwa, and wanted..." I swallowed hard. "We hadn't settled on a name. I wanted to, but Anwa was more...cautious. Then she miscarried and said that was how things were meant to be. But she was at fourteen weeks, so we'd started to tell people." I rubbed my face. "I was so damn excited, and then...she dumped me. Took the miscarriage as a sign we weren't meant to be together. Returned the ring I'd given her and asked me to lose her number."

"Jesus."

"Yeah, just about. Something..." I blinked rapidly. "I think something broke inside me. Carly approached me a couple of weeks later. I..." I rubbed my face. "I told everyone I was relieved at not being a father, and then I started dating someone who..." I sighed. "Well, Carly's nothing like Anwa. In fact, Anwa was the one who was not like the others. She was a PhD student in biochemistry at UBC. Was a research assistant on some big project. We met accidentally, hit it off, and I kind of thought it was fate when she got pregnant. I think we could've made a life together." I gestured for him to hand me the photo back.

He slowly tucked it into the envelope and with gentleness, pushed it back across the table.

When I reached for it, he placed his hand over mine.

My gaze shot to his.

His eyes were a little misty—much like mine. "Thank you for sharing that with me. That couldn't have been easy."

I sniffed. "Even Isaiah and Roger don't know the whole story. I couldn't—" I blew out a shaky breath. "—I have a reputation to uphold."

"Perhaps." He offered a soft smile. "Or maybe you're not that guy anymore. Maybe dating Anwa, and losing the baby, helped you grow up. Carly was part of your old persona—and so, at first, she felt comfortable. But you've outgrown that life. It doesn't fit anymore. Clearly, that came to a head tonight."

"She didn't take it well."

"That doesn't surprise me. She said she expected you to propose soon."

"Oh fuck." I sipped the whisky, enjoying the burn. I'd hopped a bus, so if I got shit-faced, I didn't care. Jacks was open late on Friday nights.

"Well, clearly you did the right thing by ending it." Yardley offered what I'd term a sympathetic smile. "Not that there's ever a good time."

"Yeah."

My phone buzzed in my back pocket, but I ignored it.

Then it buzzed six more times in succession.

"I apologize." I pulled it out of my pocket and checked the notification screen.

And groaned.

Yardley arched an eyebrow.

"Sorry." Even as I said the words, I tapped on the notification from Roger telling me to *not* check my notifications. *Yeah, right.*

Even as I scrolled, my heart sank.

"Carly?"

I met Yardley's gaze.

"Yeah. It's...bad." Best I could tell, she'd done a rant on Insta telling everyone what a bastard I was, and she'd tagged every member of the team who had an account.

Yardley placed his hand over mine. "Think very carefully about what you do next. Your first instinct might not be the right one."

"You mean defending myself?" My hand shook.

"Remember to consider the source. I'm sorry to say people will judge, but Carly's portrayed herself a certain way and garnered a specific type of following—those who love drama. You've been trying to be more—" He appeared to consider. "—serious. You posted about the clinic, even though you didn't mention the kids by name. Which was appreciated. You've posted a lot about Isaiah and Travis. LGBTQ-friendly stuff. You've reached people, and you probably don't even realize. Reacting in anger—or frustration—to her, won't stand you in good stead.

My phone buzzed again.

Roger. Telling me to assure him I was okay.

I typed out a quick message that I was. That I was with Yardley, and I wouldn't do anything stupid.

He gave me the thumbs-up and then ordered me to put my phone away.

Probably the toughest thing I've ever done.

I powered my phone down, then put it in my back pocket.

After all, I was sitting across from one of the nicest people I'd ever met. I'd deal with Carly's screed in the morning.

Chapter Nine

Yardley

R elief washed over me as he put his phone away. I couldn't stop him from doing something hotheaded and stupid tomorrow...but I could prevent him from doing that tonight. "Tell me about your dreams."

He blinked. "My what?"

"Your dreams? I assume playing professional rugby's one of them. Otherwise I'd have to wonder why you put yourself through that physical torture every day. How's the knee?"

He shook his leg out. "Good to go." He scratched his nose. "Yeah, pro rugby was my dream from an early age. As soon as my uncle introduced me to it. I might've thought he'd be into football—the world kind..."

I knew he meant soccer, so I nodded.

"But he really was into rugby. He was...I don't want to say a violent man. He never raised a hand to me. But he was a brutal man. A cruel man. He loved...well, violence. He loved when guys got hurt. I didn't as much, but I pretended I did. Anyway, he got me signed up and playing early on. Best thing he ever did for me. Well, that, and insisting I finish high school. He didn't think I'd be good for much other than playing, but he figured I needed some kind of education behind me."

"Did you ever go to university?"

He pursed his lips. "Uh, no. I took a few courses at BCIT. This and that. Mostly to keep me busy."

The British Columbia Institute of Technology, hmm? He'd piqued my curiosity. "What kinds of classes?"

"I messed around with some marketing stuff. I dunno, I thought I could work on improving rugby's reputation."

"Sounds noble."

"Well, I've never had the guts to talk to our front office about it. I just, like, did some projects. I was also looking at maybe taking an accounting class—I'm good at math. But they seemed hard, and I was working all the time in my courier job while trying to make the squad. Then I did—so I set my sights on the national team."

I cocked my head.

He waved me off. "They had an amazing hooker back when I was first starting, and they've had two exceptional guys since. I don't stand a chance of making the team."

"Have you tried?"

"Did you know the New Zealand All Blacks tried to recruit Isaiah? He's half Kiwi. But he would've had to prove himself in the junior leagues before he could move up, and he was better off sticking with Canada because, as good as he is, his odds of making the New Zealand team weren't great. And, by then, he'd sort of fallen in love with Travis. Plus, his mum's here, and then he and Travis bought a house—"

"Johnnie."

"Yeah?"

"Have you tried for the national team?"

"I want to. I really do." He rubbed his face. "I know I'm under consideration. But I'm getting older—"

"You're thirty-one."

"My body's been through a lot. I'm no spring chicken."

"You've got experience and grit. That's worth a lot."

"Can we change the topic?"

"Sure." For the first time, I sipped my ginger ale. All the ice had long melted. "What do you want to talk about?"

He bit his lower lip before settling those sky-blue eyes on me. "You."

I snickered. "I'm an open book. Boring as shit. Next topic."

"No, I mean it. You were married for, how long?"

"Almost fifteen years."

"Were you happy?"

I hesitated. "I thought I was. But even if he hadn't cheated on me, I wouldn't have shouted from the rooftops how lucky I was to have found the perfect man."

"The foot doctor."

"The foot doctor. Who makes a shit ton of money and who never understood the nobility of teaching."

"But teaching is noble. How will the next generation fare if we don't have great teachers?"

"His thoughts exactly."

Johnnie frowned.

"So he felt I should be teaching at the local private academy—the kids who were destined to be the next generation's top minds." I took another sip.

"But you want to help the kids who don't have all those advantages."

"Nailed it in one." I ran my hand through the condensation on my glass. "We struggled growing up. Sheer grit and determination got Jamilla through law school and me through teacher's college. Part-time jobs, scholarships...anything we could do. But that's tough terrain to navigate. If I can help my students get through it—get over it and to the other side, why wouldn't I do everything in my power? And yeah, I'm idealistic. You'd think after almost two decades that I'd know better."

"There have been successes, though, right?"

"Yep. Five kids made the Canadian Football League. Three got scholarships to US colleges, and one made the NFL. Two made it to pro hockey, and one played for the Seattle baseball team for a while. I went down to watch him for a game." I took a breath. "A couple of wrestlers, a kid who did judo—obviously didn't learn that from me—as well as a swimmer. Oh, and a diver. Which is like totally nuts. She did the ten meter, and holy shit, that's high. I've also helped kids get academic scholarships. Anything that might get them out of where we are. You know what it's like. We both straddle the downtown east-side—you from the west and me from the east. That level of poverty and deprivation..."

He nodded.

"But I've had students die. A couple in crashes, several overdoses, a couple of suicides..." I took another sip. "More good stories than bad, but that's been damn hard work on my part. Nicholas never understood that."

"Silver spoon?"

"Yep. Med school entirely paid for by his family. He graduated debt-free, while I had a pile of loans."

"Don't suppose he offered to help you pay those off."

I snickered. "Uh, no. But I didn't contribute as much to the house while I worked my ass off to clear my debts. He tried to bring that up in the divorce proceedings—claiming I should only be entitled to one-third of the house since he'd paid more for it."

"How'd that go over?"

"The mediator gently suggested he take that idea and shove it up his ass. He was on her bad side from day one—and they're not supposed to have a bad side. My lawyer advised me to keep my mouth shut and let Nicholas sink himself. Which he did. I got half of everything."

"With which you bought your house."

"I did." I grinned. "I actually like it. I wish I had more space when Jamilla comes over, but I'm just grateful she does."

He cocked his head.

"With the size of her house, it's entirely conceivable she'd never want to visit my little place. But she finds my place *charming,* and one or more of my nephews stays over a couple of times a month. The attic's configured with beds for all of them. So they've got their own space."

"But you could convert it to bedrooms for your own kids, right?"

My breath caught. My heart stuttered. My chest tightened. "I don't have kids, Johnnie."

"Well, no. I get that. But you clearly want them. But Nicholas didn't, right? Or am I reading between the lines and getting it wrong?"

Shit. "You're..." I took a deep breath. "Even Jamilla doesn't know—"

"That you want kids? It seems pretty obvious to me—"

"How badly I wanted them. I was always able to make excuses that, I think, sounded plausible."

"Or she was oblivious to your pain."

I didn't like that he thought Jamilla might not care. Or that she might not know what was in my heart. "I talk a good game, Johnnie. Almost as good as you."

He tipped his whisky glass at me. "Touché."

I took another sip of my drink. "Yes, I wanted kids. But I'm too old now—"

He snorted.

I glared.

"Who just told me I wasn't too old for the national team?"

"Well, you're thirty-one."

"And thirty-nine is not too old to be a father. Hell, men in their fifties and sixties father babies. Although admittedly not generally with women that old. Biology's weird that way."

I squinted. "That women in their sixties can't have biological children?"

"That men in their sixties can. There should be a cutoff. I mean, if you're sixty-five and father a kid, you might not even be around for their graduation. I take issue with that."

"Uh...okay. That's fair. But doesn't the same apply for a thirty-nine-year-old?"

"So you'd be forty when the kid's born. Fifty-eight when they graduate from high school. Like sixty-something when they finish university. They have kids, and you're a grandpa before you're seventy. That's not so bad."

I sighed. "You make it sound so easy. Just find a woman, get her pregnant, have a baby..."

"There are, like, adoption sites, right? For pregnant women who want to give their babies up for adoption?"

"And they'd pick a single gay man? Over a family?"

He pursed his lips. "What about kids who're already born? They need homes too."

"Again, single gay man." *Why am I arguing? Yes, I might be able to become a foster parent...but that's a remote possibility.*

"That's bullshit." He spat out the word.

The women in the booth next to ours glanced over.

I tried to duck.

Johnnie leaned forward. "Sorry to have disturbed you."

"No worries."

He cleared his throat. "Are you Julie Reyes?"

At that, my gaze shot to two women next to us, and holy shit, Julie Reyes was in the booth next to ours.

She grinned. "I'm trying to keep a low profile, but yes, that's my name."

I might not have recognized her, if not for Johnnie's keen observation.

The actress's normally distinctive white-blonde hair was secured under a baseball cap. The bill was low, shadowing her distinctive emerald-green eyes.

Trust Johnnie to have recognized the well-known celebrity. She starred in a television show about a superhero. She was his nemesis. The villain Lyric.

She pointed to her friend. "This is Lindy."

The woman with tan skin waved enthusiastically.

I wracked my brain, thinking I'd seen her somewhere as well. "I'm Yardley, and this is my friend Johnnie."

"We're mates." Johnnie indicated between the two of us.

Friends...mates...yeah, we were becoming those.

"Johnnie's a rugby player with the Vancouver Orcas." Because offering him up to two gorgeous women seemed like a logical thing to do. Everything I'd read about Julie Reyes, including that she was single—I thought—said she was a super-nice person. She and Johnnie would make a striking couple. All blond god and goddess.

"I'm not much of a rugby fan, sorry." She appeared genuinely apologetic for that.

"No worries. Violent sport." He leaned toward the women. "Super awkward here, but Yardley has three nephews, and I mean, who isn't a Justice fan?"

Vigilante Justice was the name of the show she worked on, and Justice was the superhero character played by the swoon-worthy Cole Hamilton.

"Are you fishing for an autograph?" Julie laughed.

"It would make him the best uncle ever."

"Sure." She dug around in her handbag and came up with a notepad and a sharpie. "How many nephews? One for each? And you'll want Lindy to sign some as well."

Lindy tried to wave her off.

Julie glared. "Stop being like that. You're a big star too."

The pieces fell into place in my mind. Lindy Doshi. She'd had supporting roles in several big films over the past few years.

I grinned. "I loved you in that movie with Cole Hamilton and Peter Erickson. You were amazing." Cole and Peter had played gay lovers in the bittersweet film. Peter had won the Academy Award for that little movie.

Lindy's dark-brown eyes flashed gratitude. "Yeah, that was a great film."

Ten minutes later we had five autographs secured from each woman—one for each of my nephews plus one for myself and one for Johnnie.

Julie and Lindy promised to watch the next rugby match, but I certainly wasn't going to hold them to it.

They resettled, and I eyed my watery ginger ale.

"I still say *bullshit*." Johnnie met my gaze with flinty blue eyes.

I blinked. And tried to replay our previous conversation in my mind. "Fostering and adopting is harder for single people—especially gay, single men."

"I don't think you want it enough." He downed the last of his whisky and shot a look over his shoulder.

The adorable bartender grinned and nodded.

Less than a minute later, another whisky appeared.

Johnnie grinned. "He's a fan."

"Ah."

"I still pay for my drinks."

"Julie Reyes just paid for hers. If she doesn't get comped, I didn't figure you would."

Johnnie laughed. "Some people are more into sports than movie stars."

"Have you *seen* Julie Reyes?" I might be gay, but I knew drop-dead gorgeous when I saw it. And she'd been really sweet, giving us all those autographs. We'd certainly tried to give her a graceful way out, but she'd insisted that anyone who shouted *bullshit* and played rugby deserved something.

My companion had blushed.

We'd accepted the autographs. Meyer wouldn't care, but both Roland and Kolson were huge *VJ* fans—never missing an episode. Roland was a little young to understand the *will they or won't they* sexual tension between Cole and Julie's characters, but Kolson understood. He'd made a couple of comments about bisexual Cole's appearance that had hit my radar. I'd made certain, with Jamilla's knowledge, that Kolson and I had a conversation about it being okay to like boys, girls, enbies, or all of the above.

He'd rolled his eyes.

I vowed to pay better attention.

"I've seen Julie Reyes." He glanced toward the door she'd just disappeared out of. "I've also seen you." He turned his attention back to me. "You want kids. Why not make it happen?"

Chapter Ten

Johnnie

S tupid.

    I wasn't supposed to call myself stupid. If I caught any of my teammates referring to themselves as stupid, I would've knocked them upside the head.

But *stupid* was the only word I could come up with.

I'd hurt Yardley. I hadn't intended to do that...but I had.

Just...he so clearly wanted kids. My heart had broken for him. Much as it did every time I studied the ultrasound of my daughter, taken just a couple of weeks before she died.

I tucked the envelope back at the bottom of the junk drawer, then tossed my jacket on the couch.

Then picked it up, took it to the closet, and hung it up.

My fingers itched to check my phone, but I'd promised both Roger *and* Yardley that I wouldn't until morning.

I didn't *need* my phone. Nothing was ever critical. No one ever *needed* me. I was just the guy to grab a drink or chum around with. For important stuff, we all turned to Roger. As elder statesman, and father of five, he knew how to keep everyone in line and what needed to be done in a crisis.

Unlike me, who could barely remember to make certain my socks matched.

Because, frankly, who gave a shit if they didn't?

Clearly not me.

But if my kid's socks were mismatched? I'd worry people thought I wasn't a good dad. And I wanted to be the best dad ever.

Since that was never going to happen, and being proud I'd lasted six minutes without my phone, I snagged it from my back pocket and powered it up.

Yeah, it exploded with notifications.

Swiping to literally delete them all, I searched for my address book. I found Yardley's number and hit call.

Shit. He's driving, you fuckwit.

He'd dropped me off seven minutes ago.

"Are you okay?" His voice came through the line, a little muffled. "Did you check your notifications?"

"I did not." I puffed my chest out, even though he couldn't see. "Are you driving?"

"Hands free. Through the speaker system in the SUV. I'm at a red light on Québec Street."

"That can be dangerous."

"I've passed Science World. I'm at East 5th."

"Oh." He'd made it out of the craziest part of the downtown. "Well, okay, then."

"Why did you call me, Johnnie? Because it's only been five minutes—"

"Nine minutes," I corrected him. "Maybe even a bit longer...?"

A long pause.

"I didn't think you'd had that much to drink." A wry tone.

"Wouldn't I be having a more difficult time telling time if I'd had more to drink?" That sentence made way more sense in my head than when I spoke it aloud. I wasn't anywhere near drunk. Not with just two whiskies and a plate of shared nachos onboard. After I'd made my insensitive comment, Yardley had flagged down a server, and we'd shared a plate of nachos—extra jalapeños and cheese.

Thank God he wasn't wussy with spicy foods.

"Are you okay? That's my question. Do you need me to turn around? I'm happy to do it, Johnnie. I'll be there if you need me."

I'll be there if you need me.

That was something like what Isaiah said to people when they were hurting.

Those words never came easily to me.

"I'm okay." I blew out a long breath. "I didn't check my notifications. I literally deleted all of them."

"Good for you." He sounded genuinely enthusiastic about it. "Tomorrow you can get a summary from someone—"

"You?"

A pause. "Well, I was thinking someone who knows you better. Like Isaiah or Roger."

"I don't want to bother them. Shit, that sounds bad." I pressed my hand to my forehead.

"How does it sound bad?" Vague amusement.

"That I don't mind bothering you, but I don't want to get them any more involved than they already are. You know what I mean?"

"I do."

A siren wailed in the distance.

I moved toward my window, wondering if it might be outside, but I quickly realized the noise came from the phone. "Are you being pulled over?" My heart sped up. Driving while Black was a thing. What if Yardley got pulled over by some asshole, racist—

"Going the other way and passing me now." He chuckled. "I'm a very boring driver who drives a very boring SUV who never speeds."

Ah. So he'd read my mind. I hated that we even had to think about it, frankly.

"I'll get the lay of the land and call you in the morning."

"Right."

"Are you going to be okay until then? I'm serious about turning around. I mean, you could always come and stay at my—"

"Really?"

"Sure." He said the word slowly. "My place is very boring, Johnnie."

"Yes, but it's not *here*. It still feels like she's you know, going to leap out of the closet or something." Perhaps an exaggeration, but the clutter she'd brought in here was in a box by the front door. If I wasn't environmentally oriented, I'd just haul the thing down to the dumpster and leave it there.

"I'm making a right on East 12th and I'll loop back around. Be in the lobby of your condo in twelve minutes."

"That's weirdly specific."

"I'm just looking at how long we've been conversing and counting backward. I can do math while driving, I'll have you know."

"Yeah, okay. Uh...thanks."

"My pleasure. Fair warning—I'm a grump before my first cup of coffee." He cut the line.

I made a beeline to my bedroom where I grabbed a duffel bag. Without overthinking things, I packed enough clothes for two nights. Because, fuck, I didn't want to be here this weekend—especially if shit was raining down.

Eleven minutes later, I was down in the lobby.

Yardley pulled up.

I sprinted out and hopped into his front seat.

Once I had my seatbelt secured, he pulled back onto the street. "Do you need me to stop anywhere?"

"Like for what?" I wracked my brains.

"I have no idea—which is why I'm asking. There's a 7-11 a few blocks from my house."

"Well, I packed condoms. I always pack condoms."

"Did you just…" He sputter-laughed. "I did not need to know that."

"I'm very conscientious about protection. That's important."

"If you say so." He hung a left back onto Hastings Street.

"I do say. You're a gay man—how can you not be conscientious about protection?"

"I didn't say I wasn't. But I'll admit I don't pack condoms with me all the time. Actually, it's good you brought them because I don't think I have any in my house, and if you decide to bring a hookup back to my house, I'd like to think you're being safe." Slowly, he drove through the intersection at Abbott Street.

Although people wandered up and down the street, no one stepped in front of us. *How many of these people are addicts? How can they fall that far? How am I any different from them?* I didn't do hard drugs. In the offseason I might do a hit of pot. But no one here grew up saying *I'm going to be a drug addict.*

"Nothing to say?" Yardley chuckled. "I haven't even asked if you're on a hookup site."

"I've barely booted Carly from my bed, and she's in full revenge mode. You honestly think I'd just hop into bed with someone else?"

"Wouldn't you? That's your reputation."

I would hop into your bed if you asked.

My brain screeched like a needle skidding across a record.

What the actual fuck? You're not gay. You've never thought of a guy that way before.

True.

But I've been thinking of Yardley that way. Wondering what it would be like to be...with him.

I took a breath. "No, reputations aren't always reality. I'm not going to have sex with someone a few hours after I broke up with the last person."

"Glad to hear it." He turned onto Québec Street. "I'm planning to crash—it's been a long day."

"Thank you for coming to my game."

He cut me a look.

"Thank you for putting up with Carly."

He snorted.

"Thank you for not making me be alone tonight."

"You only had to ask, Johnnie." He cocked his head. "Which you basically did, so here I am. Are you going to be okay?" He drove past Science World.

"I'm always okay."

He sighed. "That's a flippant answer. We both know when things didn't work out with Anwa that you weren't *okay*. You've been with Carly for a while. Breaking up has to have an impact."

"Yeah...relief and joy. I was with her for six months. That was five months and twenty-nine days too long." I angled my head, so it pressed back against the headrest. "I knew better. But it felt like everyone else was paired up, and I wasn't, and I wanted what they had."

"Was Makwa single?"

"Yep. And now he's seeing Louella." *Shit. I probably wasn't supposed to say anything. Especially to Yardley.*

"Well, if it's what Louella wants, I'm happy for them. Not a couple I would've seen coming in a million years."

"What if I'd asked Louella out?"

He cut a sharp glance at me before returning his attention to the road. "You wanted to?"

"Nope. Lovely woman, truly, but not for me."

"Who would be for you?" He stopped at the red light. Traffic whizzed across Broadway in both directions.

I drew in a sharp breath. "I don't know. I mean, does anyone ever know the true person they're meant to be with before they meet them? I mean..." I scratched my chin. "I want to say, personality. But that means I'd have to get to spend time with someone in a private setting, because who they are in front of other people might not be their true selves. Or, hell, they might always hide who they really are. They might be a manipulative person who is..." I floundered. "I should've broken up with her months ago."

"No sense regretting what you did or didn't do. You're out and that's that. Tomorrow we'll deal with the fallout on social media."

"You make it sound so easy."

"Because it is. Nothing's unrepairable. Nothing's impossible to work through and past."

"Unforgiveable sins exist."

He skirted from The Kingsway onto Fraser Street. "Sure. Like murder. Like intentionally hurting someone in some terrible way. But breaking up with someone doesn't count, okay?"

"Okay."

"Are we stopping?"

"No, thank you."

"Because you've got condoms." Said with a wry tone.

"Because I've got condoms." Said with enthusiasm.

"God, you're precious."

As I chanced a glance at him, he grinned.

I might just be okay.

Chapter Eleven

Yardley

How Johnnie Leclerc wound up in my bed was quite beyond me, but as I roused on Saturday morning, I was aware of two distinct things—his arm around my waist as he pressed against me, and the fact we both had morning wood.

Mine wasn't surprising—I was in bed with a man who, despite all my efforts to the contrary, I found attractive.

His was…unexpected.

"You smell good." He nuzzled his nose into my neck.

I froze.

How…?

Oh, right.

He'd been distressed about the breakup and the fallout. He'd said he didn't want to be alone.

I'd taken that literally and had invited him to my bed. Platonically, of course. In truth, I'd never shared a bed with anyone except Nicholas.

Until last night.

Until this morning.

"I can hear you thinking, Yardley."

Okay...well at least he doesn't think I'm Carly. That's something...right?

"Consent's a thing." He pressed a kiss to my neck.

I'd specifically worn a T-shirt and sleep pants in deference to having a guest in the house. When I was alone, I preferred sleeping naked. "What am I consenting to?"

He stilled. "I guess...did I read this wrong? Are you not attracted to me? Because I'm sure as shit attracted to you."

Again, I stilled. "Are you straight?"

He chuckled. "Yeah, that was my first thought too. I mean, I can look at Louella and think *there's an attractive woman*. I can look at you and think *what would it be like to have my cock in his mouth? Or his cock in my ass? Or my cock in his—*"

"Okay." I actually laughed. "You've made your point very effectively." And my cock was now straining under my sleep pants. "You're serious?"

"I am. I think..." He blew out a warm breath that tickled my neck. "I think I've felt this way almost from the beginning. I found out you were gay, and unlike my reaction to knowing Isaiah was gay, which was *oh, cool...he plays professional rugby and he's out*, was, instead like *holy fuck, that guy is so hot and he must be having sex all the time.*

I snorted.

"Hey...Isaiah, before Travis, did okay. Heck, I was always trying to set him up because I wanted him to be as happy as Roger was."

No missing that he didn't say as he was as well.

"Turned out, we were, uh, missing the mark."

I turned my head to meet his gaze.

In the dull morning light, I still spotted bright-red cheeks.

He cleared his throat. "Isaiah's a big guy. We kept trying to set him up with, well, guys who were about Travis's size."

"Okay."

"Twinks."

"Ah."

"Turns out Isaiah prefers..."

Yep, puce was a color someone could turn.

"Isaiah's a bottom?"

He cleared his throat again. "Yeah. Roger and me? We had no idea."

"That's not something all gay men advertise." And I was vaguely curious how Isaiah's teammates—and clearly his good friends—had figured out their, uh, miscalculation.

"So, like—" He rolled his eyes to the ceiling.

"Yes." Because I wasn't going to make this easy for him.

"Do you, uh...?"

"Johnnie?"

"Yep?"

"You need to look at me. If you want my naked cock anywhere near your body, we have to have this discussion."

He stared at me, his dark-blue eyes even darker than usual. "You're right."

"I'm going to tell you something that might or might not blow your mind." I paused for dramatic effect. "I'm vers."

He scrunched his nose. "Like, versatile? Like you don't mind?"

"Yep. I don't mind. I've done it both ways and enjoyed myself. My husband preferred I top—which was fine. But sometimes I like to have a man inside me and stimulating my prostate." Which hadn't happened in about a dozen years—Nicholas really preferred bottoming, and that was fine with me.

"Oh...I thought guys, like, always had a preference."

"You know that some straight guys enjoy being pegged by their female partners, right? Because prostate play is a thing."

Another frown.

On impulse, I pressed my lips to his for a quick kiss. "You're adorable and—"

He pressed his lips to mine. Then used my surprise to thrust his tongue into my mouth.

I broke the kiss only long enough to turn to face him.

He grasped my neck and dragged me closer.

I came willingly.

Despite the possibility of morning breath—although at least we'd both brushed our teeth before bed—I didn't care. He wanted me. He really wanted me. I wasn't a replacement for Carly—which would've been ick. No, as he pressed his hard cock against my hip, a shiver ran up and down my spine.

Yeah, he was all in for this.

So was I. I pulled back. "Can I touch you?"

"Oh God, yes." He yanked his sleep pants right off.

I replicated his actions, frustrated at how long it took. When I was free of my pants, I took a moment to yank my shirt over my head. Today called for serious skin-to-skin action.

He did the same.

We came together.

To my surprise, he grasped my cock. "You're going to have to help me." He said the words through gritted teeth. "This is new for me."

"Me too." I offered a wicked grin. "I've never been with a bi guy before. Or one who is a virgin...in certain aspects."

"You're going to be the death of me."

"I hope not." I grasped his hand and guided him to touch me. "But I prefer lube if you're going to jack me off."

"Or I could give you a blow job."

My cock jerked at the suggestion. "You don't—"

"I want. I've wanted to for...well I want to say weeks, but we both know that isn't true." His gaze held mine. "Since last night. When I shared all my crap, and you just...were so compassionate. And I thought *here's an amazing person, and I'm attracted to him, but he's a guy, so I won't do anything.* Plus, I wasn't certain you wanted more from me."

"I do. Trust me." I could admit I'd admired him from the moment he'd arrived at the school. And how, in time, I'd seen through his arrogance. To the wounded soul beneath. But now wasn't the time for confessions like that. "You're sure about the blow job?"

He was already scooting down. He pushed the covers back, and a rush of cold air hit us.

I preferred to keep the temperature chilly at night when I'd burrow under the duvet and sleep lovely dreams.

He confessed to preferring super warm, but had agreed to try it my way.

Now the cold air hit my nipples and my cock, and I gasped.

"Oh geez." He grinned. "I guess I'll just have to warm you up." He positioned himself between my spread thighs, then he took my cock in his hand, holding it firmly at the base. He tilted his head and furrowed his brow as if trying to solve some complex problem.

Don't ask him if he's sure. Don't offer him the out. He'll speak up if he's not comfortable. Of this, I had no doubt. He was a bull in a china shop when he wanted to be. And delicate and gentle other times. He was such a contradiction to me that sometimes he left my head spinning.

He lowered his mouth and licked the drop of precum from my tip. My cock jerked.

He grinned, catching my gaze. "I think you like that."

"I do. I really do." I grasped my sheets with my curled fingers.

He nibbled his way from my root to my crown. Then he pulled me into his mouth. He didn't try to go to fast, as I'd worried he might. He swirled his tongue around me, sending pleasure singing through my veins.

I wasn't going to think about how long it'd been for me. Because that wasn't what mattered. This beautiful man was sharing something special with me, and this meant more than anything.

He pulled me in farther, deep throating me.

Pleasure again shot through me. For a beginner, he was fucking good at this. Or he was just replicating what other women—

Nope. Not going there. I hadn't with Nicholas—much—and I wouldn't now.

He tongued my slit. Something that always sent me careening right over the edge. "I'm coming."

He sucked harder.

I took that as permission and spurted into his mouth.

He swallowed as I continued to empty inside him.

The moment felt suspended in time. I'd been his first. And I hadn't been entirely teasing. I'd never been with a guy who'd only been with women. I'd wondered how this might go and, in the end, it'd been better than I could have expected.

My doorbell rang.

Johnnie pulled off. "What the hell?"

"Probably a canvasser for the local politician. Can I do you next?"

The doorbell rang again.

"Shit." I rolled out of bed. "Coming!" I shouted the word, not even certain the person could hear me. I grabbed my discarded jeans and yanked them on—barely missing my cock as I zipped them up. I snagged a clean henley from my drawer as I bolted from the room. "What the fuck?" I glanced at the fireplace mantel clock.

Seven twenty-eight.

Late for me for a Saturday. Often, I had a tournament or something or just I was up.

The doorbell rang again.

I threw it open without even checking, stopping short. "Hugo?"

"Hey." He rubbed his hands together. "Can I come in?"

"Sure. Are you okay?"

A blast of cold air followed him in as he stepped into the house. So much for an early spring.

"Yeah."

I shut the door. "Where's Axel?"

"In bed. Asleep. With Midnight to keep him company."

Their Samoyed.

"Do you want coffee? I haven't made a pot yet."

He stopped his forward momentum toward the kitchen. Finally, he really looked at me. "Oh shit. You were in bed."

I chuckled. "Whatever gave you that idea?"

"I'm sorry. This was a really bad—"

I propelled him toward the kitchen. "I have pods. Coffee in mere moments." Sometimes he preferred tea, but boiling a kettle would take too fucking long. "Have a preference for flavor?"

"Do you have vanilla sweetener?"

"Of course." I always kept some on hand for my best friend. I guided him to the kitchen table, then headed to the coffee maker.

"You should at least put slippers on."

My friend knew me well. "Let me get the coffee brewing and then I will."

"Do I get to meet him?"

"Huh?" I blinked.

"The guy whose jacket is on the coatrack? Christ, I hope I didn't cockblock you."

Heat crept into my cheeks. Fortunately, my dark skin tended to hide that little problem. Unlike my best friend whose skin showed every shade of blush.

As does Johnnie's.

"He might not want to come out."

"I can go—"

"Nope. You're here now. He can choose whether he comes out or not. Are you okay sharing whatever brought you here this morning, or do we need privacy? If I ask, he'll respect it."

"Doesn't matter."

I cocked my head.

He waved me off.

I finished setting the machine and then hotfooted it back to the bedroom.

Johnnie sat on the bed, putting his socks on. He eyed my feet. "Those must be cold."

"Hence me coming to get my slippers." For just the briefest of moments, I considered stripping and putting on underwear because commando wasn't my favorite state of dress. Judging that would take too long, and after putting on my slippers, I reached out.

He'd finished putting on his socks, so he grasped my hand.

"Do you want to come and meet my best friend?"

"Does he know about us?"

"I haven't told him…" I took in a deep breath. "But he knows me and is, like, almost positive I haven't been with anyone since my ex."

"Which you haven't."

"Which I haven't. That's why he's so surprised I have a guest." I rubbed his hand. "He offered to leave, but I've asked him to stay. He has something on his mind, and I'm not certain what it might be. But that doesn't mean you have to come out to see him. You're welcome to stay here, or I can arrange for a cab to take you—"

"It's okay." He smiled. "I like the idea of meeting your friend." He ducked his head. "I like the idea that I mean something to you. I do, right?" He gazed at me earnestly.

"You absolutely do mean something. I don't just bring everyone to my bed platonically and let them give me a blow job."

He burst out laughing. "Hey, didn't say you were cranky before your first cup of coffee?"

"Normally." I winked. "But not when I get a blow job before getting out of bed. Let's go." I tugged him toward the door.

He came willingly.

We walked the short distance to the kitchen where Hugo sat at the table with his coffee.

My two traitorous cats were devouring their food. Clearly they remembered my friend was an easy mark and, just as clearly, he remembered how much to feed each one. Purrs abounded.

To my surprise, he rose when he saw Johnnie, and held out his hand. "Hugo."

Johnnie released my hand and took Hugo's. "Johnnie."

Hugo grinned. "I'll bet there's a story here—and you don't have to share. I'm just supercurious."

"Yeah, I'd be if one of my mates suddenly turned up at some guy's place when I thought he was straight."

"Uh, okay." Hugo's eyebrows shot almost to his hairline.

Johnnie laughed.

I headed to the coffee machine. "Do you want a cup?"

"Hell fucking yes." Johnnie moved toward me. "Can I help?"

I waved him off. "Won't take more than a minute. Have a seat. You're the guest."

He plopped down next to Hugo, then pointed to me. "So how did you become mates?"

"Teaching buddies. I was an old pro when this guy started."

I rolled my eyes. "Three years, my friend. You weren't an expert."

"Yeah, but I knew where the staff room was, which days to stay away from the cafeteria, and the best parking spots to avoid getting bird poop on your car." He grinned devilishly. His red hair gleamed in the sunlight streaming in the kitchen window, and his blue eyes—a shade lighter than Johnnie's—sparkled.

"All true." I finished the coffee Hugo'd started. I gestured to Johnnie.

"Black is fine."

"Okay." I walked the mug over to him, handed it over, and headed back to the machine. At this point, I was getting desperate for my own cup.

"We hit it off on day one. We were both gay, which we each picked up on quickly, but neither of us was particularly *out*. In the end, when Yardley got married, he came out."

"And survived the shitstorm." I eyed the hot, black liquid pouring into my mug.

"I survived my marriage." Hugo winced. "That ended, and I didn't see the point of coming out. Then I was outed—"

"By your future fiancé."

"—by my future fiancé." He chuckled. "Which is another story for another day. So, like, that was that. I was out, I was engaged, and this guy's marriage had just fallen apart." He winced. "Which super sucks but Nicholas was always an asshole."

"You never said." My chest squeezed.

"You were happy—at least for the first few years. Or I perceived you were happy."

"I was." I closed my eyes for a moment, then opened them. My gaze traveled back and forth between my two guests. "Or I told myself I was."

"I get that." Johnnie glanced down at his coffee. "I really do."

My coffee finished brewing. Thank God I liked things hot and was immediately able to take a swig. "So, we're not here to rehash my marriage." I eyed Hugo.

"I'm getting married in six days."

"I'm aware. Since I'm your best man and all." *Let him come to you. He never responds well to pressure tactics.*

He fingered the handle of his mug. "I don't want to think I'm making a mistake."

My heart skipped a beat. "Do you think you're making a mistake?"

"No." Said quietly with a bit of force.

"Okay." I moved to the table and sat in the chair between the two men.

"I just...what if I'm not good enough? He's Axel Freaking Townsend and—"

"Holy shit." Johnnie's jaw dropped. "You're marrying Axel Townsend? From Grindstone?" He narrowed his gaze. "Oh, wasn't there some scandal last year? Sorry, I didn't pay attention, and you probably don't want to rehash it, and why don't I just shut my mouth?"

Hugo chuckled. "Yes, *that* Axel Townsend. Yes, *that* scandal. Yes, *these* fears."

Here, I could offer support. "Hugo."

"Yeah?"

"I've never seen a man more besotted than Axel."

He arched an eyebrow.

"Yes, I just used a big, fancy word. Because it fits. He's head over heels in love with you. He professed his love for you on stage."

"Well—"

"He moved in with you."

"Well—"

I glared.

"What? He and Ed were selling the condo because Ed was buying a house with Thornton, and yes, *that* Ed Markham." He directed his comment to Johnnie.

"You're just getting cold feet. You're almost fifteen years older than him—of course you're having second thoughts." I needed him to know I understood.

"He could snap his fingers and have any man or woman he wanted."

"He couldn't have me." Johnnie grinned.

Hugo cocked his head.

"I only want him." Johnnie pointed to me.

Heat flared in my cheeks as Hugo gazed speculatively between the two of us. "I'm really sorry to have interrupted."

"No worries. He'll give me a blow job later." Johnnie sipped his coffee. "Do you have any cookies to go with this? I'm starving."

Hugo smacked his palm against his forehead. "I left the donuts in the car. One moment." He stood and hurried out of the kitchen. A moment later, the front door slammed shut.

"Uh, Johnnie...?"

"Yep." He grinned.

Because he knew exactly he was doing.

And he was daring me to question him about it.

"How do you like your eggs? Because donuts don't have enough protein for a professional athlete."

He continued grinning. "Over easy—like me."

An hour later, Hugo left—after having secured a promise from Johnnie that he'd be my plus-one at the intimate ceremony to be held six days from then.

I couldn't believe it.

How is this my life?

Chapter Twelve

Johnnie

Axel and Hugo's wedding wasn't at all what I expected.

First, the hesitant Hugo was completely absent. When he was told he could *kiss the groom,* he pulled Axel into a massive bear hug and kissed him until Ed finally tapped Axel on the shoulder and whispered something.

The lead bassist from Grindstone had his hair in dreads and a huge grin on his face as he interrupted the sucking of face.

Axel, after hearing whatever his best man whispered, pressed a kiss to Hugo's cheek, then turned the two of them to the small crowd gathered.

A cheer went up, which I participated in enthusiastically.

Hugo's niece and nephews sauntered over to him. His eldest niece and nephew offered hugs, while the younger middle child headed for Axel and clearly demanded a hug.

Hugo's sister, Leonora, was speaking to her husband when their little girl, Mia, headed for the melee.

Yardley swooped in to save her from being trampled and hoisted her into the air.

She giggled.

Her mother pivoted and smiled. "Thank you."

Four kids. What an insane brood.

I'd kill for just one. I'd be grateful for just one.

One felt like asking too much, though, in that moment.

Yardley caught my gaze. His smile was wistful.

I nodded, understanding. We were both in our thirties—me early and he later—with no prospects of becoming fathers. Yet we both wanted to be.

Big Mac and Meg, two members of Grindstone, approached Axel. Big Mac held a baby in his arms.

So many kids. Because of my rawness—after having shared my pain with Yardley last week—I was seeing children everywhere.

"You're holding up well."

A smooth voice caught my attention, and I pivoted to find a stunning woman watching me. "I'm sorry?"

"Things can get chaotic around the band." The woman held out her hand. "Pauletta. I'm the manager."

"Ah, Johnnie. I'm the, uh, friend of the best man."

If she repped the band, she knew I wasn't referring to Ed, Axel's best man.

"You play rugby."

I cocked my head.

She laughed. "You think I didn't do background checks on everyone invited?"

Of course she did.

I winced.

Again, she chuckled. "I know revenge when I see it. Clearly, uh, your ex is..."

"Yeah."

"Well, the fury's mostly died down. That's good, given how long stuff like this can last."

"I'm...what would you say, a B-list celebrity at best?"

"Rugby's getting to be more popular. You've got some talented people in your front office who are doing some top-notch marketing. Personally, I'd love to see Grindstone sing an anthem you guys use for your ads."

I blinked. "Really?"

She eyed me. "I'm planning to make some calls. I'll admit it hadn't occurred to me before, but after having gone down a rabbit hole investigating you, I can see the upside for both the band and your team. No idea if your people will agree."

"I don't have any influence over them. I wish I did..."

"That's okay. No worries." She appeared very unruffled.

"And you think the band would be interested?"

"If the right opportunity comes along, I'd convince them. In truth, everyone's intrigued by Hugo's best friend's invite. Lots of speculation."

"Hugo hasn't said anything?"

"Hugo can be very tight-lipped when he wants to be. We also know when not to pry." She gazed toward the happy couple and their entourage. "They're protective of their own. Yardley is in the circle now that Hugo's fully inside, if you know what I mean."

"Are you warning me?" Part of me was amused, and part of me was damn wary. This woman looked like she could eat me for breakfast then use my bones to floss her teeth.

"Paulie?" Another attractive person with a shock of red hair approached Pauletta from behind.

My instinct was to gender them, but I tried not to. See? I could learn.

"Mickey, sweetheart." Pauletta put her arm around the person, and they made a striking couple with the manager's dark skin and the other person's paler complexion. "This is Johnnie. Yardley's...friend."

Yeah, okay, I'd kind of walked into that one.

"Johnnie, this is my partner, Mickey."

I extended my hand.

Mickey shook with a tight grip. They smiled. "Are you prepared for a party?"

"Uh...sure."

Both Axel and Ed had been sober for almost a decade, so no booze or pot tonight. Just good old-fashioned *fun*.

Mickey chuckled. "You have no idea what you're in for."

"Nope. Not a clue."

When Yardley and I stepped into the house late that night, my feet ached, I was a little woozy from lack of sleep—we'd had an early practice this morning—and on a natural high from just having had so fucking much fun.

"You're okay with me staying the night?" I could've gone home. My car sat parked in his driveway since we'd gone together in his SUV so as to not take up an extra parking spot at Ed and Thornton's house—where the celebration had taken place. Their extensive estate had easily accommodated the band, roadies, partners, and Hugo's family.

Axel didn't have any blood relatives—just the members of his band.

"Why didn't Hugo have more teaching friends?" He'd only brought Yardley and two others. I toed off my shoes since my host hadn't said anything about me not staying. The twenty-minute drive home felt insurmountable. God, I was exhausted.

"They wanted to keep the gathering intimate." Yardley bent over to untie his laces, affording me the most awesome view of his ass.

After Hugo had cockblocked us last weekend, we hadn't started up where we'd left off.

I'd called Roger, who'd looped in Isaiah and Jason, and the four of us gathered for drinks at Jacks to strategize how I'd survive the shitstorm.

In the end, doing nothing had been the answer.

As Pauletta said, things had just...blown over.

Carly wasn't as hot shit as she thought she was, and even her five-hundred thousand followers weren't all that sympathetic to her clear attempts to take me down.

My seventy-five thousand followers rallied around me and offered support.

The local media hadn't even poked their heads above the parapet in interest. Now, if I'd been a Canuck or a Lion, things would've been very different. Pro hockey and football were next level. Soccer too.

Pauletta hadn't been wrong, though, when she suggested rugby was picking up traction in Vancouver and elsewhere in Canada.

"Did you know Grindstone's manager suggested the band record an anthem for my team?" I hung my suit jacket on the coatrack. The thing was a little worse for wear and would require dry cleaning. Oh well, having toddler Mia's chocolate-covered fingerprints all over the thing was totally worth it.

That child had zero fear of strangers, and when she decided she really liked my man bun, that had been that. She'd spent about ten minutes trying to pull it free.

I brushed the hair from my eyes now.

God only knew what'd happened to the elastic after she threw it off into the plants in the garden where we'd taken a stroll.

To get some fresh air and to get away from the chaos of the party.

She's appeared to enjoy herself—in her yellow frilly dress.

"I think that's an awesome idea." Yardley rubbed his eyes. "But I don't know how that would happen."

"Me either—but I gave her the name of our publicity director. I'm certain she could've found it herself, but I wanted to seem like I was helping, you know?"

"Because it's a great opportunity?" He hung his suit jacket over the back of a kitchen chair. "Okay, I want a shower and then to crawl into bed and sleep for a month."

"Sounds good. You mind if I use your guest bathroom?"

"Nope. Have at it. And if we're quick, there should be enough hot water. I keep meaning to get an on-demand system, but it's never a priority. My downstairs tenant has her own tank, so I never have to worry."

"I can be quick." For the first time in a week, I ventured into his personal space. I snagged him around the waist and pulled him close. "Kiss?"

"Thought you'd never ask."

I cocked my head. "Why didn't you say something?"

He eyed me. "Hugo railroaded you into coming tonight. I wasn't going to assume we were on a date. You were being a friend and keeping me company."

"Sure..."

"Are you ready for displays of affection?"

"I've barely figured out I like giving blow jobs." I tried for a smile.

"I'm not going back into the closet."

"Oh."

"Yeah."

What does that mean? I wanted to ask, but I was afraid to. "Does this mean I'm sleeping in your spare room?"

"It means things are complicated. But I liked being in your arms. I wouldn't turn that down again."

I'll take it. I'll take whatever I can get. "I think I left my toothbrush here."

"You did." He grinned. "And your condoms. You know where the guest bathroom is. Toothbrush is there."

"And the condoms?"

"My nightstand." With that, he sauntered away.

Great.

Except... "Hey!"

"Yeah?"

"I don't have pajamas."

"Who says you need them?" His disembodied voice carried through the house.

My cock perked up.

Well, okay then.

Chapter Thirteen

Yardley

Waking up in Johnnie's arms for the second time in a week was pretty damn sweet.

Both of us being naked was even sweeter.

He pressed his cock against my ass. "You awake?"

"Yep."

"Finally." He sighed. "Like, can we do something about this?" He pressed closer. Then he reached around and snagged my morning wood. "And this?"

I chuckled. "Keep that up and it'll be over in no time."

"Yeah? I thought you *older guys* were, uh, slower to react."

"Hey." I laughed. "I get it up just fine. Refractory period's longer."

"The what?"

"Time between going off and being able to go again."

"Ah." He rubbed his stubbled chin against my shoulder blade. "I probably knew that, but all this sex talk has me horny."

I almost made a joke about him always being horny. Except that just wasn't true. Despite his reputation, I'd seen him put so many other important, and unimportant, things before sex. I pressed my ass back against him. "You up for this?"

"Yep." Said with enthusiasm and pep.

"You think about how you want it?"

He stilled. "For this first time?"

"Yep." Repeating his word.

"Can I, uh, make love to you? I want to try it the other way—oh God, I really do—but I haven't, uh, and uh..."

I loved both his inarticulateness as well as the fact he'd never done anal before. That brought a specialness to this. An intimacy I had only dreamed of. "I'd love for you to make love to me." *Instead of saying fucking...because I want more from you.*

"Cool." He kept a firm grasp on me. "So, how does this work?"

I smiled to myself. "Uh, you stick your cock—"

He squeezed my cock.

I yelped. Then chuckled. "There's lube, condoms, and all that stuff involved."

He snorted. "I know that. I need to get tested. Repeatedly. I might've been faithful, but I'm not convinced she was."

Ouch.

"I meant...positions." He cleared his throat.

He's probably blushing. So cute.

We were still shrouded in darkness with just a bit of morning light poking through the blinds. "Are you comfortable facing me?"

"Uh...yeah..."

"Then I either lie on my back or I ride you." I bit my lower lip, waiting for his reaction.

"I can look in your eyes? See how you're doing?"

"Yes."

"Then I choose that option." He pressed another kiss to my shoulder. "But I gotta piss, and I really want to brush my teeth. For our first time."

Our first time. God, I liked the sound of that. "I'll do the same."

He leapt out of bed while I did a roll and landed with my feet on the floor. Going to bed naked—and inviting him to join me naked—had been a risk. But our relationship had reached that level of intimacy. Sure, we could've fucked our way through the week. Waiting, though, sweetened everything. We'd had glances and innuendo, but no actual contact. Almost to see if what we had was real or not.

I shuffled to the bathroom, pissed, and brushed my teeth. Coffee might not taste so good when I drank it later, but I didn't give a shit. I splashed cold water on my face, noted the couple of silver whiskers, pushed that thought aside, and headed to the bedroom.

To find Johnnie on the bed rolling a condom on his length.

"Eager?"

He grinned. "I got hard as soon as I came in. I sniffed your pillow and wow, instant boner."

I laughed. "Yeah, okay. Can't say I've ever tried that one." My cock responded to seeing the beautiful man on display. He really was stunning, with his blond hair cascading around his cheeks, over his shoulders, and even partway down his back. I'd asked about the choice, and he said he loved having his hair pulled. All the time—not just during sex.

Fully intending to take him up on that thinly veiled request, I headed to the bed. "So, on my back?"

His blue eyes lit in the dim light. "Yes, please."

I managed to position myself. I wasn't ripped like him, but I was in decent shape for a man my age. *You're not over the hill yet.* Right. A quick reminder.

He held the bottle of lube. "So..." He chuckled, but it came out a little forced. "Isaiah says Travis likes it when he preps him. When Isaiah preps Travis," he clarified.

I'd understood.

"So, do you like...?"

"Well, since it's been oh, about a dozen years, I can say either would be—"

"You're okay with it?"

"Yeah." I caressed his cheek. "I trust you. But some guys find it—"

"Not me." His eyes grew flinty. "I've spent a week doing research. I'm so fucking curious about prostates. So, I want to find yours, and then I want you to find mine."

"I can do that." I tried to hold in the grin.

He arched an eyebrow.

I laughed.

His expression morphed from mock outrage to genuine happiness in an instant. All it took, apparently, was the promise of prostate explorations.

I lay back, spread my legs, and tucked my very erect cock and my balls out of the way.

"Oh, wow. Just...wow." He ran his hands up and down my inner thighs.

After trying to hold back the reaction, I shivered. I'd spent the week longing for his touch. Now I had it, it nearly overwhelmed me. "Have at it."

"I intend to." He coated his fingers with lube and then touched my rim—gentle and soft.

Truthfully, I was okay with him taking it easy for our first time. No sense rushing things.

Slowly, he inserted one finger.

I grinned.

After poking it around for a bit, he added a second.

I nodded.

As he held my gaze, he started rotating them. Scissoring me open. Searching...

He brushed my soft, spongy spot, and I gasped, which caused him to still.

"No, that was a good reaction. Keep going." Prostate play was always tricky because I was so damn sensitive. I didn't want to go off too soon and, after all, it'd been twelve years. I'd played with myself a few times, to be sure, but my focus was always on Nicholas and his pleasure. *I was a fool, and I'm not going to think about it anymore.*

"This feels good?" Johnnie cocked his head.

"It feels fucking amazing."

He grinned. "My turn soon."

"Yep. Today. Tomorrow. Whenever you're ready." Which implied we'd be repeating this over and over—which was fine with me.

"I need to be inside you."

"Then add some lube to your cock, and let's get this show on the road." I grinned. "I can't wait."

"A dozen years, eh?"

"Yep."

"I only hope I can make it good for you."

"I'm not worried." And I wasn't. If he happened to go too rough, I'd manage. Ask him to back off. If he didn't go hard enough, I'd coax him into more vigor. The point was we'd do this together.

As I hoped we'd always be.

Chapter Fourteen

Johnnie

As I lined my cock up with Yardley's entrance, a feeling of rightness settled over me. Not only that I could do this—although that was important—but that he wasn't just a rebound. He was *Yardley*. And, despite the Carly debacle, I'd just had the best month of my life.

"You okay?" His brow furrowed in concern.

"Yeah. Truly." I pressed against him and then, inch by inch, inside him.

He hissed out a breath.

I hesitated.

"No." He nearly shouted that. "Keep going. It's going to burn because I haven't done this in forever, but it'll be fine. I'll adjust and then...magic." His eyes lit with pure pleasure. Something I didn't see enough of.

I'm going to make him smile more. I didn't know if I could, but I was damn well going to try.

The pressure on my cock was intense—as I'd known it would be—but nothing I couldn't handle. Eventually, my head popped in.

Yardley let out a little sigh of relief. "Maybe a little slow?"

"Yep." And I did plan to do exactly that. My movements were deliberate, gentle, and steady as I pressed myself farther and farther into him. As I sought his sweet spot. As I sought the place that would bring me pleasure as well. Mine was secondary, of course, but I was going to chase this orgasm for all I was worth—even knowing I might not get there. This was sex. Sex was messy. Sometimes body parts didn't do what we expected of them—what we hoped of them.

Suddenly, I was fully seated.

Again, he sighed.

Then nodded.

Okay. Showtime. I withdrew almost to the tip and pushed back in.

He grinned.

I repeated the process.

He smiled.

Again and again and again.

"You can go harder, Johnnie. I'm not going to break."

No, but I might. My heart might break wide open, and I might profess these insane feelings. I might tell you that I love you. Which is nuts...right? Yet I continued to thrust inside him—picking up the pace and the intensity as I did. The intervals shortened. Our breaths quickened.

He grasped my hair and pulled.

I moaned as my scalp tingled.

Then he snagged his cock and tugged to the timing of my thrusts. Thank fuck, because that wasn't even something I'd thought of.

"I'm coming, Johnnie. I'm..." The words trailed off as he spurted cum all over his hand. A bit of it landed on my chest, even as the orgasm I'd chased appeared quite suddenly. I thrust once more, then held myself still.

Our eyes locked.

My body stiffened as the climax overtook me. I soared high above the mountains as high as an eagle. I wanted the feeling to go on forever. The power and the might.

Yet I knew it wouldn't. It couldn't.

He exhaled.

I blew out a breath as well as my heart rate started to return to normal. Slowly, I withdrew with a little pop. I giggled.

He grinned. "Get rid of the condom, and then we'll snuggle. I want to hold you in my arms—if that's what you want as well."

"Yeah, I do."

"Great." He blinked, almost as if struggling to keep his eyes open.

I laughed. "About to fall asleep on me?"

"Late night, early morning, great orgasm? Entirely possible."

Wanting to be in his arms if he dozed off, I dispensed of the condom into his garbage can and crawled back into bed, pulling the cover over us. "So, no friends ringing the doorbell?"

"God, I hope not. They're headed out on their honeymoon."

Axel and Hugo were headed to Greece to spend time at Hugo's sister's resort. Although she, her husband, and their brood had been there yesterday, Hugo hadn't gotten quality time with them. I'd wondered about Axel's feelings at having to share his new husband, but apparently he loved his new nieces and nephews as much as Hugo did and so this was, to him, a treat. Then the couple were to fly on to England to scout out a future concert venue.

Pauletta had *plans* for the band.

Yardley banded his arm around my chest.

"Oh, what about the cats?" Because they were what was really important.

"I gave them extra kibble before bed last night. They'll survive."

Generally, they tended to be well-behaved creatures, so I trusted Yardley to know. I might sneak them an extra treat if they were good and let us rest. "Do you think they'd be good with kids?"

He stiffened. Then cleared his throat. "They're amazing with my nephews. Patient and kind, even when Meyer's trying to pull their tails. Well, he's pretty much out of that phase. In all these years, not a single scratch. Now, they're getting older..." He swallowed hard.

"I get it." I pressed my hand to his as it lay against my chest. "So are we."

"You want kids."

"I want kids. It might not happen, but—" I floundered,.

"We can make it happen. There are kids living on the streets right now that we could give a home to. They'd have huge psychological issues, but we can deal with that. Or younger kids who need a safe space for a while—maybe while their parents get their shit together. There are so many ways we can do this." His voice animated more and more as he spoke.

So much for him falling asleep. "You honestly think it'll be that easy?"

"Well, we could even look for a pregnant woman who wants to give up her baby. You know that big movie star, right? Peter Erickson? He and his husband found their daughter that way. They're really open about that and how it changed their lives. We could do that, Johnnie. I mean, not tomorrow. We'd need to get married first..."

A silence enveloped the room.

Forever, it felt like.

"Yardley?"

"Yeah?" He might've squeaked that.

"Did you just propose?"

"Too soon, right?"

"Maybe just a bit?" I smiled. "Ask me again when we're not in a post-orgasmic haze." I carefully didn't specify a timeframe. I'd leave it up to him. But hell, if he waited too long, I might do it myself. This relationship felt both incredibly rushed and incredibly right. "I will say this." I took a deep breath—sort of grateful we weren't facing each other. "I think I love you. Which is all kinds of crazy given it's been, what, a day?"

"Four weeks."

"Right. Four weeks." I smiled. "Still crazy."

"Johnnie?"

"Yeah."

"I feel the same way."

"Oh. Well, just so you didn't feel pressured—"

"Johnnie?"

"Hmm?"

"Have I ever felt pressured into doing anything?"

I thought about it for an inordinate amount of time. I wanted to be certain I reviewed our entire relationship before responding, "no."

"So when I say *I love you,* then you know I'm sincere, right? That I *do* love you?"

"Well, when you put it like that..."

He kissed my shoulder.

"Rest now, sweetheart. We've got all the time in the world." Today was Sunday, and we had the day off. Then balls-to-the-wall practices until our big game on Friday night against Montréal. We *had* to break our losing streak against them. We just had to.

And, on that note, I drifted off to sleep.

Chapter Fifteen

Yardley

"How do you stand this?" I shouted in Becca's ear.

Roger's wife offered me a broad grin. "You just do. Don't you get nervous when your students play? Compete?"

I pressed a hand to my roiling stomach. "Well, frankly, no. They'll do their best and—

Dead ball. Another scrum.

Except time was running out. Vancouver was behind by three points and needed to score. Crunch time.

Both teams positioned themselves over the ball and began the process of pushing each other.

Although I understood rugby, some things eluded me. Like scrums. Like running the ball sideways.

Like the no protective gear.

Roger'd taken another hard hit, and Becca stressed about his shoulder until Francine gave him the okay and he'd charged back into the game.

Montréal grabbed the loose ball, and before Vancouver could really mount a defense, the Québecers had the ball over the line.

Three quarters of the stadium groaned while a small group of die-hard Montréal fans cheered their hearts out.

Time elapsed, and the game ended.

"Come on." Becca grabbed my hand.

"What...?" I barely had time to respond before she was hauling me along the row and then down the aisle. "Aren't we supposed to meet them in the waiting area?" At least that's where I'd met Johnnie before. When Carly had been there. Bit of a catastrophe, that night.

Yeah, but you're here now, and she's not. She'd made her choice when she turned on Johnnie. People broke up. Hell, he might dump me. Didn't give me the right to attack him on social media or impugn his reputation. He hadn't cheated on her. He'd stayed faithful. He'd also realized their relationship needed to end. And ended it had—in spectacular fashion.

The security guard took one look at the charging Becca and, bright man, stepped aside. Of course, she'd been coming here forever, and apparently most of the staff knew her.

Roger spotted her and strode over, scooping her into his arms and kissing her fiercely.

Isaiah headed our way and belatedly I realized Travis was behind me.

Another emotion-laden reunion. These guys had played their hearts out, but beating Montréal just seemed out of their reach.

"Yardley!" Johnnie shouted my name.

He ran over, and nearly knocked me over as he wrapped his arms around my neck.

Right there, on the field, he kissed me for all he was worth.

Despite the general noise, Becca's cheer, as well as the hoots and hollers from the rest of the team permeated my kiss-drunk senses.

He pulled back. "I should lose more often."

"I don't care. I mean, obviously—for your sake—I'd prefer you win. But I'd love you either way."

A camera flash went off.

We turned.

The photographer grinned at Johnnie. "Who's this?"

Johnnie continued to hold me. "Yardley Morrison. He's my boyfriend."

My heart melted.

Epilogue

Johnnie

"You may kiss the groom." The priest beamed as he offered the words.

Isaiah grasped Travis's cheeks in his hands and pressed the sweetest of kisses.

Had that been me? I'd have kissed Yardley for all I was worth.

As if sensing that, he grasped my hand.

The grooms before us, though, had to be more circumspect. Isaiah's mother had spent a lot of time cajoling her church to let her baby boy get married here—in a space she held close to her heart. The battle had been an uphill slog, but she'd won. This was the first gay wedding to be held here and, we all hoped, not the last.

Becca, who stood to my right, sniffed.

Roger, catching his wife's eye from the riser, smiled. He'd been happy to stand up for Isaiah. Travis's friend Dodge was standing up for him. I'd yet to hear the story behind the name—because his given name wasn't *Dodge*, but I hadn't figured it out yet.

Something for later?

Yardley squeezed my hand.

"You are now married." The priest raised his hands toward the grooms.

The room erupted in laughter, cheers, and applause.

The man appeared momentarily taken aback.

Ah, no one warned him what a squad of rugby players and their spouses were like.

Fair.

The grooms started back down the aisle, but stopped at the first pew where both kissed Isaiah's mom. The mom who had always embraced him, loved him, and championed him. And she now loved her son-in-law just as fiercely.

Love I'd never known.

Still, if not for my uncle and his love of rugby, I wouldn't have made it into Yardley's life, and mine would have been so much poorer. Would I have figured out I was bi? Hard to say. Did I love having his cock up my ass? Hell fucking yes.

The grooms passed us, with Travis winking at me.

I might've picked his brain about how to be a good bottom. Turned out, laying there and taking it wasn't all I could do. I'd used his advice and had blown Yardley's mind.

Go me.

Roger extended his hand to Becca.

She offered him a brilliant smile.

They walked down the aisle together.

I sighed.

Yardley pressed himself against me. "What?"

"I want that." I gestured with my chin.

"Five kids and a house in the suburbs?"

"Burnaby?"

"Yeah."

"That would be a bitch of a commute for both of us."

"Yeah."

"But your house has three spare bedrooms for kids. Why would we move?" Plus, if things got really nuts, we could reconnect the basement to the main house and use it as part of our home instead of a rental unit.

"So let's not move. Except to get the last of your stuff in with me."

I was happy to walk away from my rental apartment in Gastown. The landlord had a waiting list a mile long and was thrilled to return my security deposit and to see the last of me. Probably planned to jack up the rent. Unfortunate for the next person—but at least they'd have a roof over their head. "Sounds good."

We followed the crowd out to the little reception area where hugs were given freely. I loved that about the squad—the affection shared easily with everyone.

Hell, even Yardley gave more than a few hugs.

Two hours later, our asses were parked in a line near the buffet at a local celebration hall.

I hopped from foot to foot.

Yardley pressed a hand to my hip. "You look like you have to pee."

"I'm hungry." That might've contained the hint of a whine.

Travis and Isaiah made their way, along with Isaiah's mother, to the front of the line.

Isaiah caught my gaze.

I nodded.

He grinned and cleared his throat. "I know you're all starving—"

A cheer went up.

"—but we have one last thing to take care of."

General good-natured grumbles.

There, in front of my entire squad, their families, and everyone else invited—about sixty people—I dropped to one knee.

Isaiah's mother gasped.

Becca squealed.

Yardley's inhale was sharp.

I grasped his hand. "I know—" *Remember to breathe.* "—we talked about you proposing."

A general chuckle went up.

"But I needed you to know that I'm in this too. That I want to show you how much I love you. And yeah, it's only been two months—"

"And six days." He added that because precision was important to him.

"And six days," I repeated. I fumbled in my pocket for the ring. When I finally had a good grasp on it, I held it out. "Would you do me the honor—" I couldn't. My throat closed with an emotion so strong it would've brought me to my knees had I not already been there.

He lowered himself so he knelt across from me. "From the moment you stepped into my gym, I thought *that's a guy I could love.* Not just because you're sexy as fu—"

I grinned.

He cleared his throat. "But because you have a heart of gold. Those kids look up to you, and they're lucky to have you in their lives." His eyes shone.

I read the unspoken words as well—that if we ever had kids of our own, whatever that looked like, they'd be lucky too.

"You're mine." He grasped my chin and kissed me something fierce. His tongue invaded my mouth as I clung to him—ever mindful of the ring.

Finally, he pulled back. "The answer's yes."

"Oh, thank God." Roger laughed. "Now can we eat?"

That night, as Yardley and I came together, we pledged ourselves to each other. This was a forever thing.

Out of disaster, I'd found my forever man.

Thank you for reading *Big Rucking Disaster!*
Check out the rest of our amazing Rugby Romances in this series!
Hot Rucking Canadian
Arrogant Rucking Player
Sweet Rucking Temptation
Star Rucked Lovers
Playing Rucking Hard
Friends Rucked Up
Revamped Rucking Reaper
Big Rucking Deal

Want more Gabbi Grey?
Check out her Love in Mission City series, set in beautiful British Columbia.
The first book is
Ginger Snapping All the Way (Love in Mission City Book 1)

Also available:

Stanley's Christmas Redemption(Love in Mission City Book 2)(Love in Mission City Book 2)

The Beauty of the Beast (Love in Mission City Book 2.5)

Sleigh Bells and Second Chances (Love in Mission City Book 3)

A Daddy for Christmas 2: Foster (Love in Mission City Book 3.5)

Rayne's Return (Love in Mission City Book 4)

Gideon's Gratitude (Love in Mission City Book 5)

Love in Mission City: The Boyfriend Gamble

Love in Mission City: The Four Seasons

Love in Mission City: The Boyfriends Duet

Love in Mission City: The Shorts

Puppy Pride

Rayne Check

Archer's Awakening

Leo's Lust

A Daddy for Christmas 3: Lorcan

Thought You Were the One

Love Without Reservations

Page Against the Machine

The Lightkeeper's Love Affair

Ace's Place

Marcus's Cadence

Not in it for the Money

Also:

Axe to Grind

Grindstone's Edge

Voice to Raise

Hugh (Single Dads of Gaynor Beach)

Anthony (Single Dads of Gaynor Beach)

Xavier (Single Dads of Gaynor Beach)

Love Furever (Friends of Gaynor Beach Animal Rescue)

Husky Love (Friends of Gaynor Beach Animal Rescue)

Yorkie to My Heart (Friends of Gaynor Beach Animal Rescue)

A Furever Home (co-written with Kaje Harper – Friends of Gaynor
Beach Animal Rescue)

My Past, Your Future

If Only for Today

Catch a Tiger by the Tail

Solstice Surprise

Valentino in Vancouver

You See Me

Sun, Surf, and Surprises

Ginger in the City

Caressa's Homecoming (Bound by Love Book 1)

Cole's Reckoning (Bound by Love Book 2)

An Uncommon Gentleman

A Sensible Gentleman

Didn't See You Coming

Finding Noah (Foggy Basin Season 2)

Unlocked and Unlost

Hot Rucking Canadian

Big Rucking Disaster

Audiobooks

Ginger Snapping All the Way

Stanley's Christmas Redemption

Sleigh Bells and Second Chances

Rayne's Return

Gideon's Gratitude

Rayne Check

Archer's Awakening

Thought You Were the One

Love in Mission City: The Shorts

Page Against the Machine

The Lightkeeper's Love Affair

Ace's Place

Marcus's Cadence

Not in it for the Money

Hugh (Single Dads of Gaynor Beach)

Anthony (Single Dads of Gaynor Beach)

Love Furever (Friends of Gaynor Beach Animal Rescue)

Husky Love (Friends of Gaynor Beach Animal Rescue)

My Past, Your Future

If Only for Today

Catch a Tiger by the Tail

Solstice Surprise

An Uncommon Gentleman

A Sensible Gentleman

Didn't See You Coming

Want a free short story? The story is set in Gaynor Beach, California where there are plenty of single dads and puppy rescues! You can sign up for my newsletter so you can keep up with all the great stuff I'm doing as well as pictures of my own pooches, Ally and Finnegan.

Hemingway's Happy Day

Love contemporary MF romances? What's better than love in the
beautiful Cedar Valley in British Columbia, Canada? Find small town
romances with a touch of angst, a bit of heat, and a lot of heart...

The Absolution of Abigail Reardon (prequel)
The Luminosity of Loriana Harper (Book 1)
The Making of Marnie Jones (Book 2)
The Redemption of Remy St. Claire (Book 3)

Interested in knowing more about Gabbi?

Sign up for her newsletter
Follow her on Bookbub
Follow her on Instagram

USA Today Bestselling author Gabbi Grey lives in beautiful British Columbia where her fur baby chin-poo keeps her safe from the nasty neighborhood squirrels. Working for the government by day, she spends her early mornings writing contemporary, gay, sweet, and dark erotic BDSM romances. While she firmly believes in happy endings, she also believes in making her characters suffer before finding their true love. She also writes m/f romances as Gabbi Black and Gabbi Powell.